Georges Simenon was born at Liège in Belgium in
1903. At sixteen he began work as a journalist
on the *Gazette de Liège*. He has published over
180 novels in his own name, sixty-seven of which
belong to the Inspector Maigret series, and his
work has been published in thirty-two languages.
He has had a great influence upon French
cinema, and more than forty of his novels have
been filmed.

Simenon's novels are largely psychological. He
describes hidden fears, tensions and alliances
beneath the surface of bourgeois family life, which
suddenly explode into violence and crime. André
Gide wrote to him: 'You are living on a false
reputation – just like Baudelaire or Chopin. But
nothing is more difficult than making the public
go back on a too hasty first impression. You
are still the slave of your first successes and the
reader's idleness would like to put a stop to your
triumphs there.... You are much more important
than is commonly supposed', and François
Mauriac wrote, 'I am afraid I may not have the
courage to descend right to the depths of this
nightmare which Simenon describes with such
unendurable art.'

Simenon has travelled a great deal and once lived
on a cutter, making long journeys of exploration
round the coasts of Northern Europe. He is
married and has four children, and lives near
Lausanne in Switzerland. He enjoys riding, fishing
and golf.

Georges Simenon

Maigret goes home

Translated by Robert Baldick

Penguin Books

Penguin Books Ltd, Harmondsworth,
Middlesex, England
Penguin Books Inc, 7110 Ambassador Road,
Baltimore, Maryland 21207, U.S.A.
Penguin Books Australia Ltd, Ringwood,
Victoria, Australia
Penguin Books Canada Ltd,
41 Steelcase Road West,
Markham, Ontario, Canada
Penguin Books (N.Z.) Ltd,
182–190 Wairau Road,
Auckland 10, New Zealand

L'Affaire Saint-Fiacre first published in France 1931
Published by A. Fayard et Cie 1959
Maigret and the Countess published in
England in the volume *Maigret Keeps A
Rendezvous* by Routledge Kegan Paul Ltd 1940
This translation first published in Penguin Books 1967
Reprinted 1970, 1972, 1974, 1976
Copyright © Librairie Arthèmes Fayard, 1959
Translation copyright © the Estate of Robert Baldick, 1967

Made and printed in Great Britain by
Hunt Barnard Printing Ltd, Aylesbury
Set in Linotype Times

1 The Little Girl with the Squint

A timid scratching at the door; the sound of an object being put on the floor; a furtive voice:

'It's half past five! The first bell for Mass has just been rung ...'

Maigret raised himself on his elbows, making the mattress creak, and while he was looking in astonishment at the skylight cut in the sloping roof, the voice went on:

'Are you taking communion?'

By now Chief-Inspector Maigret was out of bed, standing barefoot on the icy floor. He walked towards the door, which was closed with a piece of string wound round a couple of nails. There was the sound of footsteps hurrying away, and when he got out into the corridor he was just in time to catch sight of the figure of a woman in a spencer and a white petticoat.

Then he picked up the jug of hot water which Marie Tatin had brought him, closed his door, and looked for a piece of mirror in front of which he could shave.

The candle had only a few minutes of life left. Outside the skylight, it was still night, a cold night in early winter. A few dead leaves were clinging to the branches of the poplars in the market place.

Maigret could stand up only in the middle of the attic, because of the double slope of the roof. He was cold. A thin draught of air, the source of which he had been unable to trace, had chilled the back of his neck.

But it was precisely this quality of coldness which

disturbed him, by plunging him into an atmosphere which he thought he had forgotten.

The first bell for Mass ... The bells ringing out over the sleeping village ... When he was a boy, Maigret did not usually get up so early ... He would wait for the second bell, at a quarter to six, because in those days he did not need to shave ... Did he so much as wash his face?

Nobody brought him any hot water ... Sometimes the water was frozen in the jug ... Soon afterwards his shoes would be clattering along the hardened road ...

Now, while he was getting dressed, he could hear Marie Tatin coming and going in the main room of the inn, rattling the grate of the stove, moving crockery about, and turning the handle of the coffee-mill.

He put on his jacket, his overcoat. Before going out, he took out of his wallet a piece of paper with an official slip pinned to it bearing the words:

Municipal Police of Moulins.
Communicated for information and possible action to Police Headquarters in Paris.

Then a sheet of squared paper ... Laborious handwriting:

This is to tell you that a crime will be committed in the church at Saint-Fiacre during the first Mass on All Souls' Day.

*

The sheet of paper had lain around for several days in the offices of the Quai des Orfèvres. Maigret had noticed it by accident, and had asked in surprise:

'Is that Saint-Fiacre near Matignon?'

'Probably, seeing that it was sent to us by Moulins.'

And Maigret had put the piece of paper in his pocket.

Saint-Fiacre. Matignon. Moulins. Words which were more familiar to him than any others.

He had been born at Saint-Fiacre, where his father had been the steward of the château for thirty years. The last time he had gone there had in fact been after the death of his father, who had been buried in the little graveyard behind the church.

A crime will be committed . . . during the first Mass . . .

Maigret had arrived the day before. He had taken a room at the only inn in the village: Marie Tatin's. She had not recognized him, but he had recognized her because of her eyes. The little girl with the squint, as they used to call her. A puny little girl who had become an even skinnier old maid, squinting more and more, and endlessly bustling about the bar-room, the kitchen and the yard where she kept rabbits and hens.

The chief-inspector went downstairs. The ground-floor rooms were lit by oil-lamps. A table was laid in one corner. Coarse grey bread. A smell of coffee with chicory, and boiling milk.

'You're wrong not to take communion on a day like today. Especially seeing that you're taking the trouble to go to the first Mass . . . Heavens! That's the second bell ringing already!'

The voice of the bells was faint. Footsteps could be heard on the road. Marie Tatin fled into her kitchen to put on her black dress, her cotton gloves, and her little hat which her bun prevented from staying on straight.

'I'll leave you to finish your breakfast . . . You'll lock the door, won't you?'

'No, wait! I'm ready . . .'

She was embarrassed to be walking along with a man. A man who came from Paris! She trotted along, a small bent figure, in the cold morning air. Some dead leaves were fluttering about on the ground. The crisp sound they

7

made showed that there had been a frost during the night.

There were other shadowy figures converging on the dimly shining doorway of the church. The bells were still ringing. There were some lights in the windows of the low-built houses: people dressing in a hurry for the first Mass.

And Maigret rediscovered the impressions of his childhood: the cold, the eyes smarting, the tips of the fingers frozen, a lingering taste of coffee in the mouth. Then, on going into the church, a wave of warm air, of soft light; the smell of the tapers and the incense . . .

'Excuse me, will you? . . . I've got my own prayer-stool,' she said.

And Maigret recognized the black chair with the red velvet armrest of old Madame Tatin, the mother of the little girl with the squint.

The rope which the bell-ringer had just let go of was still quivering at the far end of the church. The sacristan was lighting the last tapers. How many were there in that ghostly gathering of half-asleep people? Fifteen at the most. There were only three men: the sacristan, the bell-ringer, and Maigret.

. . . a crime will be committed . . .

At Moulins the police had treated the matter as a bad joke and had not worried about it. In Paris, they had been surprised to see the chief-inspector set off.

Maigret heard some noises behind the door on the right of the altar, and he could guess second by second what was happening: the sacristy, the choirboy arriving late, the priest putting on his chasuble without a word, joining his hands together, and walking towards the nave, followed by the boy stumbling along in his cassock . . .

The boy was red-haired. He shook his bell. The murmur of the liturgical prayers began.

8

. . . during the first Mass . . .

Maigret had looked at all the shadowy figures one by one. Five old women, three of whom had a prayer-stool reserved for their own use. A fat farmer's wife. Some younger peasant-women and one child . . .

The sound of a car outside. The creak of a door. Some light footsteps, and a lady in mourning walking the whole length of the church.

In the chancel there was a row of stalls reserved for people from the château, hard stalls in old, polished wood. And it was there that the woman took her seat, noiselessly, followed by the peasant-women's eyes.

Requiem aeternam dona eis, Domine . . .

Maigret could perhaps still have recited the responses to the priest. He smiled at the thought that in the past he had preferred the Requiem Masses to the others, because the prayers were shorter. He could remember Masses which had been celebrated in sixteen minutes . . .

But already he had eyes only for the occupant of the Gothic stall. He could barely make out her profile. He hesitated to identify her as the Comtesse de Saint-Fiacre.

Dies irae, dies illa . . .

It was she, all right! But when he had last seen her she was twenty-five or twenty-six. She was a tall, slim, melancholy woman whom he used to catch sight of from a distance in the park.

And now she must be well into the sixties . . . She was praying fervently . . . She had an emaciated face, and long delicate hands which were clasping a missal . . .

Maigret had remained in the last row of straw-bottomed chairs, those which cost five centimes at High Mass, but were free at Low Masses.

. . . a crime will be committed . . .

9

He stood up with the others at the first Gospel. Details attracted his attention on all sides and memories forced themselves upon him. For example, he suddenly thought:

'On All Souls' Day the same priest celebrates three Masses . . .'

In his time, he used to breakfast at the priest's house, between the second and third Masses. A hard-boiled egg and some goat's cheese . . .

It was the Moulins police who were right. There couldn't be a crime!

The sacristan had taken his seat at the end of the stalls, four places beyond the countess. The bell-ringer had walked away with a heavy tread, like a theatrical producer who has no desire to watch his own production.

There were no men left but Maigret and the priest, a young priest with the passionate gaze of a mystic. He didn't hurry like the old priest the chief-inspector had known. He didn't mumble half the verses.

The stained-glass windows were turning pale. Outside, day was breaking. A cow was lowing on a farm.

And soon everybody was bending double for the Elevation. The choirboy's bell tinkled shrilly.

Maigret was the only one who did not take communion. All the women walked towards the altar rail, their hands folded, their faces expressionless. Hosts so pale that they seemed unreal passed for a moment through the priest's hands.

The Mass continued. The countess's face was buried in her hands.

Pater Noster . . .
Et ne nos inducas in tentationem . . .

The old woman's fingers parted, revealed a tormented face, opened the missal.

Another four minutes . . . The prayers. The last Gospel. And then everybody would go out. And there wouldn't have been a crime.

For the warning stated clearly: *the first Mass* ...

The proof that it was over was that the sacristan was standing up, was going into the sacristy ...

The Comtesse de Saint-Fiacre's head was buried in her hands once more. She was not moving. Most of the other old women were just as rigid.

Ite, missa est ... The Mass is over ...

Only then did Maigret feel how anxious he had been. He had scarcely realized. He heaved an involuntary sigh. He waited impatiently for the last Gospel, thinking that he was going to breathe the fresh air outside, see people moving about, hear them talking about this and that ...

The old women woke up all together. Feet shuffled about on the cold flag-stones of the church. One peasant-woman made for the door, then another. The sacristan appeared with a candle extinguisher and a thin wisp of blue smoke took the place of each flame.

Day had broken. Grey light was entering the nave at the same time as draughts of air.

Three people were left ... Two ... A chair moved ... Only the countess remained and Maigret's nerves went taut with impatience ...

The sacristan, who had finished his task, looked at Madame de Saint-Fiacre. A puzzled expression passed across his face. At the same moment the chief-inspector stepped forward.

There were two of them standing close to her, surprised at her immobility, trying to see the face which was hidden by the joined hands.

Suddenly alarmed, Maigret touched the shoulder. And the body tipped over, as if it had been balanced on a knife's edge, rolled on to the floor, and lay motionless.

The Comtesse de Saint-Fiacre was dead.

*

The body had been taken into the sacristy where it had been laid on three chairs placed side by side. The sacristan had run out to fetch the village doctor.

As a result, Maigret forgot how unusual his presence was. He took several minutes to understand the suspicious inquiry in the priest's burning eyes.

'Who are you?' the latter finally asked. 'How is it that . . .'

'Chief-Inspector Maigret, from Police Headquarters.'

He looked the priest in the eyes. He was a man of thirty-five, with features which were regular but so solemn that they recalled the fierce faith of the monks of old.

He was profoundly disturbed. A somewhat unsteadier voice murmured:

'You don't mean that . . .?'

They had not dared to undress the countess. They had vainly held a mirror to her lips. They had listened for her heart which was no longer beating.

'I can't see any wound,' was Maigret's only reply.

And he looked around him at this unchangeable scene in which not a single detail had altered in thirty years. The altar-cruets were in the same place, and the chasuble prepared for the following Mass, and the choirboy's cassock and surplice.

The dirty light entering through a Gothic window was thinning out the rays of an oil-lamp.

It was hot and cold at the same time. The priest was assailed by terrible thoughts.

Maigret did not understand the full drama of the situation at first. But memories of his childhood went on rising to the surface like air bubbles.

. . . A church in which a crime has been committed must be newly consecrated by the bishop . . .

How could there have been a crime? Nobody had heard a shot. Nobody had approached the countess.

During the whole Mass, Maigret had scarcely taken his eyes off her.

And there was no sign of bloodshed, no visible wound.

'The second Mass is at seven o'clock, isn't it?'

It was a relief to hear the heavy tread of the doctor, a red-faced fellow who was impressed by the atmosphere and looked in turn at the chief-inspector and the priest.

'Dead?' he asked.

All the same, he for his part did not hesitate to un-button the countess's bodice, while the priest turned his head away. Heavy footsteps in the church. Then the bell which the ringer had set in motion. The first bell for the seven o'clock Mass.

'I can only suppose that heart failure ... I wasn't the countess's regular doctor. She preferred to be attended by a colleague in Moulins ... But I've been called two or three times to the château ... She had a very weak heart ...'

The sacristy was tiny. The three men and the corpse could only just fit inside. Two choirboys arrived, for the seven o'clock Mass was a High Mass.

'Her car must be outside,' said Maigret. 'We must arrange for her to be taken home ...'

He could still feel the priest's anguished gaze weighing on him ... Had he guessed something? The fact remained that while the sacristan, with the chauffeur's help, was carrying the body to the car, he came over to the chief-inspector.

'You're sure that ... I've another two Masses to say ... It's All Souls' Day ... My parishioners are ...'

Seeing that the countess had died of heart failure, wasn't Maigret entitled to reassure the priest?

'You heard what the doctor said ...'

'All the same, you came here today, to this particular Mass ...'

Maigret made an effort not to get flustered.

'Just a coincidence, Monsieur le Curé ... My father

is buried in your graveyard ...'

And he hurried out to the car, an old model, whose chauffeur was turning the starting-handle. The doctor did not know what to do. There were a few people on the square who could not make out what was happening.

'Come with us ...'

But the corpse took up all the room inside. Maigret and the doctor squeezed inside next to the back seat.

'You look surprised at what I told you,' murmured the doctor, who had not yet completely recovered his composure. 'If you knew the situation, you might understand ... The countess ...'

He fell silent, glancing at the liveried chauffeur who was driving his car with an absent-minded expression. They crossed the sloping square, which was bordered on the one hand by the church built on the hillside, and on the other by the Notre-Dame pond which, that particular morning, was a poisonous grey colour.

Marie Tatin's inn was on the right, the first house in the village. On the left was an avenue of oaks, and, right in the distance, the dark mass of the château.

A uniform sky, as cold as an ice-rink.

'You know, this is going to create some complications ... That's why the priest looked so upset.'

Doctor Bouchardon was a peasant, and the son of peasants. He was wearing a brown shooting-outfit and high rubber boots.

'I was off duck-shooting in the ponds ...'

'You don't go to Mass?'

The doctor winked.

'Mind you, that didn't stop me being on good terms with the old priest ... But this one ...'

They were driving into the park. Now they could make out the details of the château, the ground-floor windows covered by their shutters, and the two corner towers, the only old parts of the building.

14

When the car drew up near the steps, Maigret looked down through the latticed windows at ground level and caught a glimpse of the steam-filled kitchens, and a fat woman busy plucking partridges.

The chauffeur did not know what to do, and did not dare to open the car doors.

'Monsieur Jean won't be up yet ...'

'Call somebody ... anybody ... There are some other servants in the house, aren't there?'

Maigret's nostrils were moist. It was really cold. He remained standing in the courtyard with the doctor, who started filling a pipe.

'Who is Monsieur Jean?'

Bouchardon shrugged his shoulders and gave a queer smile.

'You'll see.'

'But who is he?'

'A young man ... A charming young man ...'

'A relative?'

'If you like ... In his own way ... Oh, I might as well tell you straight away ... He's the countess's lover ... Officially, he's her secretary ...'

Maigret looked the doctor in the eyes, remembering that he had been at school with him. But nobody recognized him. He was forty-two. He had put on weight.

As for the château, he knew it as well as anybody else. Especially the out-buildings. He only had to take a few steps to see the steward's house, where he had been born.

Perhaps it was these memories which were disturbing him so much. Especially the memory of the Comtesse de Saint-Fiacre as he had known her: a young woman who, for the country boy he had been, had personified all that was feminine, graceful and noble.

And now she was dead. They had bundled her like an inanimate object into the car, and they had had to bend her legs. They had not even buttoned up her bodice and some white underwear was poking out of the mourning dress.

... a crime will be committed ...

But the doctor maintained that she had died of heart failure. What supernatural power had been able to foresee that? And why call in the police?

People were running about inside the château. Doors were opening and shutting. A butler who was only half-dressed opened the main door a little way, hesitating to come out. A man appeared behind him, in pyjamas, his hair tousled, his eyes tired.

'What is it?' he called out.

'The pimp,' the cynical doctor growled in Maigret's ear.

The cook had been told too. She was looking silently out of her basement window. Dormer windows were opening at the top of the house, in the servants' rooms.

'Well, why doesn't somebody carry the countess to her room?' Maigret thundered indignantly.

All this struck him as sacrilegious, because it did not tally with his childhood memories. It made him feel not merely morally but physically sick.

... a crime will be committed ...

The second bell for Mass was ringing. People must be hurrying. There were farmers who came a long way, in light carts. And they had brought flowers to place on the tombs in the graveyard.

Jean did not dare to approach. The butler, who had opened the car door, stood there utterly crushed, without moving a muscle.

'Madame la Comtesse ... Madame la ...' he stammered.

'Well? ... Are you going to leave her there? ... Eh? ...'

Why the devil was the doctor smiling sarcastically?

Maigret used his authority.

'Come on now! Two men ... You' (he pointed to the chauffeur) 'and you' (he pointed to the butler) 'carry her up to her room ...'

While they were reaching into the car, a bell rang in the hall.

'The telephone ... That's peculiar at this hour,' growled Bouchardon.

Jean did not dare to go and answer it. He seemed to be in a daze. It was Maigret who rushed to unhook the receiver.

'Hullo ... Yes, the château ...'

A voice which seemed very close said:

'Will you ask my mother to come to the telephone? She must be back from Mass by now ...'

'Who's that speaking?'

'The Comte de Saint-Fiacre ... In any case, that's none of your business ... Let me speak to my mother ...'

'Just a minute ... Will you tell me where you're speaking from?'

'From Moulins ... But dammit all, I tell you ...'

'It would be best if you came over here,' was all that Maigret said before he hung up.

And he had to press against the wall to let the body which the two servants were carrying pass by.

2 The Missal

'Are you coming in?' asked the doctor as soon as the dead woman had been laid on her bed. 'I need somebody to help me to undress her.'

'We'll find a chambermaid,' said Maigret.

And, sure enough, Jean went up to the next floor and came down a little later with a woman of about thirty who cast frightened glances around her.

'Clear off!' the chief-inspector growled at the servants, who asked for nothing better.

He held Jean back by the sleeve, looked him up and down, and led him into a window recess.

'What terms are you on with the countess's son?'

'But ... I ...'

The young man was thin, and his striped pyjamas, which were of questionable cleanliness, added nothing to his prestige. His eyes avoided Maigret's. He had a nervous habit of pulling at his fingers as if he wanted to lengthen them.

'Wait!' the chief-inspector broke in. 'We're going to speak plainly, to save time.'

Behind the heavy oak door of the bedroom they could hear footsteps coming and going, the creaking of the bedsprings, and orders being given in an undertone to the chambermaid by Doctor Bouchardon. The dead woman was being undressed.

'What exactly is your position at the château? How long have you been here?'

'Four years ...'

'You knew the Comtesse de Saint-Fiacre?'

'I ... That is to say, I was introduced to her by common friends ... My parents had just been ruined by the crash of a little bank in Lyons ... I came here as a confidential secretary, to look after the countess's personal affairs ...'

'I beg your pardon. What were you doing before?'

'I travelled ... I wrote some art criticism ...'

Maigret did not smile. In any case, the atmosphere did not lend itself to irony.

The château was huge. From the outside it was fairly impressive. But the interior looked as seedy as the young man's pyjamas. Dust everywhere, old things without any beauty, a host of useless objects. The curtains were faded.

And on the walls, there were paler patches which showed that pieces of furniture had been removed. The best pieces, obviously. Those which had some value.

'You became the countess's lover ...'

'Everybody is free to love whoever ...'

'Idiot!' growled Maigret, turning his back on the other.

As if things were not obvious in themselves. You only had to look at Jean. You only had to breathe the atmosphere of the château for a few moments, and catch the servants' glances.

'Did you know that her son was coming?'

'No ... What can that matter to me?'

And his eyes still avoided Maigret's. With his right hand he tugged at the fingers of his left.

'I'd like to get dressed ... It's cold ... But why are the police bothering about ...?'

'Yes, go and get dressed.'

And Maigret pushed open the bedroom door, avoiding looking towards the bed, on which the dead woman was completely naked.

19

The bedroom resembled the rest of the house. It was too big, too cold, still cluttered up with old ornaments. Trying to lean on the marble mantelpiece, Maigret noticed that it was broken.

'Have you found anything?' the chief-inspector asked Bouchardon ... 'Just a moment ... Will you please leave us alone, Mademoiselle?'

And he closed the door behind the chambermaid, went and pressed his forehead against the window, and let his gaze wander over the park which was carpeted with leaves and grey mist.

'I can only confirm what I told you earlier. Death was due to sudden heart failure.'

'Brought on by ...?'

A vague gesture from the doctor, who threw a blanket over the corpse, joined Maigret at the window, and lit his pipe.

'Perhaps a shock ... Perhaps the cold ... Was it cold in the church?'

'Far from it. You didn't find any sign of a wound, of course?'

'No.'

'Not even the barely perceptible trace of a prick?'

'I thought of that ... No, nothing at all ... And the countess hasn't imbibed any poison ... So you see it would be difficult to maintain ...'

Maigret was frowning. On the left, under the trees, he could see the red roof of the steward's house, where he had been born.

'In a few words ... What is life at the château like?' he asked in an undertone.

'You know as much about that as I do ... One of those women who are models of good behaviour up to the age of forty or forty-five ... It was then that the count died, and the son went to Paris to continue his studies ...'

'And here?'

'Secretaries came along, who stayed for longer or shorter periods ... You've seen the latest ...'

'The fortune?'

'The château is mortgaged ... Three out of four farms have been sold ... Every now and then an antique dealer comes to collect some piece which is still worth something ...'

'And the son?'

'I can't say I know him very well ... They say he's quite a lad ...'

'Thank you.'

Maigret was going to leave the room. Bouchardon followed him.

'Between ourselves, I'd like to know how you happened to be in the church just this very morning ...'

'Yes, it's strange ...'

'I've a feeling that I've seen you before somewhere ...'

'That's possible ...'

And Maigret hurried along the corridor. His head felt a little empty, because he had not slept long enough. Perhaps he had caught cold too at Marie Tatin's inn. He caught sight of Jean going downstairs, dressed in a grey suit but still wearing slippers. At the same moment a car without a silencer drove into the château courtyard.

It was a little sports car, painted bright yellow, long, narrow, and uncomfortable. A man in a leather coat burst into the hall the next moment, pulling off his helmet and shouting:

'Hullo! ... Anybody there? ... Is everybody still asleep here?'

But then he caught sight of Maigret, whom he looked at inquisitively.

'What is it?'

'Shh ... I must have a word with you ...'

Next to the chief-inspector, Jean was pale, uneasy. As he passed, the Comte de Saint-Fiacre gave him a gentle punch on the shoulder and said jokingly:

'Still here, you little rotter?'

He did not seem to bear him any malice. Just to despise him profoundly.

'There's nothing wrong, is there?'

'Your mother died this morning, in the church.'

*

Maurice de Saint-Fiacre was thirty years old, the same age as Jean. They were of the same height, but the count was broad-shouldered and a little fat. Everything about him, especially dressed as he was in his leather coat, breathed life and gaiety. His bright eyes were gay and mocking.

It needed Maigret's words to make him frown.

'What's that you said?'

'Come this way.'

'Well, I'm damned ... And I was ...'

'You were ...?'

'Nothing ... Where is she?'

He was dazed, dumbfounded. In the bedroom he raised the blanket just far enough to see the dead woman's face. There was no explosion of grief. No tears. No dramatic gestures. Just three murmured words.

'Poor old girl!'

Jean had thought fit to come as far as the door, and the other, catching sight of him, snapped at him:

'You get out!'

He was getting agitated. He paced up and down the room and bumped into the doctor.

'What did she die of, Bouchardon?'

'Heart failure, Monsieur Maurice ... But the chief-inspector may know more about that than I do ...'

The young man swung round to face Maigret.

22

'You're from the police? ... What ...?'

'Could we have a few minutes' conversation? ... I'd like to take a little walk up the road ... You're staying here, aren't you, Doctor?'

'The fact is I was going shooting ...'

'Well, you can go shooting another day.'

Maurice de Saint-Fiacre accompanied Maigret, gazing thoughtfully at the ground in front of him. When they reached the main drive of the château, the seven o'clock Mass had just finished and the parishioners, in greater numbers than at the first Mass, were coming out and forming groups on the square. A few people were already going into the graveyard, and only their heads showed above the wall.

As the sky grew lighter, the cold became sharper, probably on account of the north wind, which was sweeping the dead leaves from one side of the square to the other, making them spin around like birds over the Notre-Dame pond.

Maigret filled his pipe. Wasn't that his chief reason for taking his companion outside? Yet the doctor had smoked even in the dead woman's room, and Maigret was in the habit of smoking anywhere.

But not in the château! That was a place apart, which throughout his youth had represented all that was most inaccessible.

'Today the count called me into his library to work with him,' his father used to say, with a hint of pride in his voice.

And the boy that Maigret had been at that time used to gaze respectfully, from a distance, at the baby-carriage being pushed around the park by a nursemaid. The baby in it was Maurice de Saint-Fiacre ...

'Does anybody stand to benefit from your mother's death?'

'I don't understand ... The doctor has just said ...'

23

He was uneasy. His gestures were jerky. He snatched the piece of paper which Maigret held out to him and which foretold the crime.

'What does this mean? . . . Bouchardon spoke of heart failure and . . .'

'Heart failure which somebody foresaw a fortnight in advance!'

Some peasants were looking at them from a distance. The two men approached the church, walking slowly, following the train of their thoughts.

'What were you coming to the château for this morning?'

'That's just what I was thinking,' said the young man. 'You asked me just now . . . Well, yes . . . There *is* somebody who stood to benefit from my mother's death . . . Me!'

He was not joking. His forehead was furrowed. He greeted by name a man who went by on a bicycle.

'Seeing that you're from the police, you must have understood the situation already . . . Besides, that fellow Bouchardon is sure to have talked . . . My mother was a poor girl . . . My father died . . . I went away . . . Left on her own, I can well believe that her mind became slightly unhinged . . . First of all she spent all of her time at church . . . Then . . .'

'The young secretaries . . .'

'I don't think it was what you think and what Bouchardon would like to suggest . . . Nothing immoral . . . Just a longing for affection . . . The urge to look after somebody . . . The fact that those young fellows took advantage of that to go further . . . Mind you, that didn't prevent her from remaining very pious . . . She must have had some terrible attacks of conscience, torn as she was between her faith and that . . . that . . .'

'You were saying that you stood to benefit?'

'You know that there isn't very much of our fortune

24

left ... And people like that gentleman you've seen have hearty appetites ... Let's say that in another three or four years there'd have been nothing left at all ...'

He was bare-headed. He ran his fingers through his hair. Then, looking Maigret in the eyes, he added after a pause:

'All that remains for me to tell you is that I was coming here today to ask my mother for forty thousand francs ... And I need those forty thousand francs to cover a cheque which would otherwise bounce ... You see how everything ties up ...'

He broke a twig off a hedge they were passing. He seemed to be making a violent effort to prevent himself from being overwhelmed by what had happened.

'And to think that I've brought Marie Vassilief with me!'

'Marie Vassilief?'

'My mistress ... I've left her in her bed at Moulins ... She's quite capable of hiring a car and driving over here ... That puts the lid on it, doesn't it?'

They were only just putting out the lamp in Marie Tatin's inn, where a few men were drinking rum. The bus for Moulins was about to leave, half empty.

'She didn't deserve that!' said Maurice's thoughtful voice.

'Who?'

'Mother.'

And at that moment there was something childlike about him, in spite of his height and slight paunchiness. Perhaps he was at last on the verge of tears.

The two men walked up and down near the church, covering the same ground over and over again, sometimes facing the pond, sometimes with their backs to it.

'Look, Chief-Inspector ... Nobody could have killed her, after all ... Or else I don't understand ...'

Maigret was thinking about that, and so hard that he

25

forgot about his companion. He was recalling every little detail of the first Mass . . .

The countess in her pew . . . Nobody had gone near her . . . She had taken communion . . . Next she had knelt down with her face in her hands . . . Then she had opened her missal . . . A little later, her face was in her hands again . . .

'Excuse me for a moment . . .'

Maigret went up the steps and entered the church, where the sacristan was already preparing the altar for High Mass. The bell-ringer, a rough peasant wearing heavy hobnailed boots, was straightening the chairs.

The chief-inspector walked straight up to the stalls, bent down, and called the sacristan, who turned round.

'Who picked up the missal?'

'What missal?'

'The countess's . . . It was left here . . .'

'You think so?'

'Come here,' Maigret said to the bell-ringer. 'You haven't seen the missal which was in this seat, have you?'

'Me?'

Either he was an idiot or he was putting it on. Maigret was on edge. He caught sight of Maurice de Saint-Fiacre who was standing at the far end of the nave.

'Who has been near this pew?'

'The doctor's wife occupied this stall at the seven o'clock Mass . . .'

'I thought that the doctor wasn't a believer?'

'He may not be. But his wife . . .'

'Well, you'll tell the whole village that there'll be a big reward for whoever brings me the missal.'

'At the château?'

'No, at Marie Tatin's.'

Outside, Maurice de Saint-Fiacre was walking beside him again.

'I can't make head or tail of this missal business.'

26

'Heart failure, wasn't it? ... That may have been brought on by a severe shock ... And it happened shortly after communion, in other words after the countess had opened her missal ... Supposing that in that missal ...'

But the young man shook his head with an expression of discouragement.

'I can't imagine any piece of news capable of shocking my mother to that extent ... Besides, it would be ... so horrible ...'

He was breathing hard. He stared gloomily at the château.

'Let's go and have a drink.'

He did not make for the château but for the inn, where his entry created a certain embarrassment. The four peasants who were drinking there suddenly felt as if they were no longer at home. They greeted the count with a respect mingled with fear.

Marie Tatin ran out of the kitchen, wiping her hands on her apron. She stammered:

'Monsieur Maurice ... I'm still all upset by the news ... Our poor countess ...'

She at least was crying. She probably wept buckets every time anybody died in the village.

'You were at the Mass too, weren't you?' she said, calling Maigret to witness. 'When I think that none of us noticed anything! It was here that I heard ...'

It is always embarrassing in such circumstances to show less grief than people who ought to be indifferent. Maurice listened to these expressions of sympathy while trying to hide his impatience, and, to keep himself in countenance, he went and took a bottle of rum from the shelf and filled a couple of glasses. His shoulders were shaken by a shudder while he drained his glass at one draught, and he said to Maigret:

'I think I caught cold coming here this morning ...'

'Everybody here has a cold, Monsieur Maurice ...'

And to Maigret she said:

'You ought to take care too. I heard you coughing last night . . .'

The peasants went off. The stove was red hot.

'A day like today!' said Marie Tatin.

And because of her squint it was impossible to say whether she was looking at Maigret or the count.

'Won't you have something to eat? I was so upset when I heard . . . that I didn't even think of changing my dress . . .'

She had simply tied an apron over the black dress she put on only to go to Mass. Her hat had been left on a table.

Maurice de Saint-Fiacre drank a second glass of rum, and looked at Maigret as if to ask him what he was to do.

'Come along!' said the chief-inspector.

'Do you want to have lunch here? I've killed a chicken and . . .'

But the two men were already outside. In front of the church there were four or five carts whose horses were tied to the trees. Heads could be seen moving over the low wall of the graveyard. And in the courtyard of the château, the yellow car was the only patch of bright colour.

'Is the cheque crossed?' asked Maigret.

'Yes. But it will be presented tomorrow.'

'Do you do much work?'

A pause. The sound of their footsteps on the hardened road. The rustle of dead leaves carried along by the wind. The horses snorting.

'I'm exactly what people mean by a good-for-nothing. I've done a bit of everything . . . Look . . . The forty thousand . . . I wanted to start a film company . . . Before that I was a partner in a wireless business . . .'

A dull explosion, on the right, beyond the Notre-Dame pond. They caught sight of a sportsman striding towards

28

the animal which he had killed and which his dog was worrying at.

'That's Gautier, the steward,' said Maurice. 'He must have gone out shooting before . . .'

Then, all of a sudden, he lost his self-control, stamped his foot, pulled a face, and nearly let out a sob.

'Poor old girl!' he muttered with his lips drawn back. 'It's . . . it's so disgusting . . . And that little rotter Jean who . . .'

As if by magic, they suddenly saw the latter pacing up and down the courtyard of the château, side by side with the doctor, and obviously talking excitedly, for he was gesticulating with his thin arms.

In the wind, every now and then, they could catch the scent of chrysanthemums.

3 The Choirboy

There was no sunshine to deform the pictures, no mist either to blur the contours. Everything stood out with cruel clarity: the tree-trunks, the dead branches, the pebbles, and above all the black clothes of the people who had come to the graveyard. The whites, on the other hand, tombstones or starched shirt-fronts or old women's bonnets, took on an unreal, deceptive value: whites which were too white and seemed out of place.

Without the dry north wind which cut your cheeks, you might have thought that you were under a rather dusty glass cloche.

'I'll see you again later . . .'

Maigret left the Comte de Saint-Fiacre outside the gate of the graveyard. An old woman, sitting on a little bench she had brought with her, was trying to sell some oranges and chocolate.

The oranges were big and ripe and frozen . . . They set the teeth on edge and rasped the throat, but, when he was ten years old, Maigret used to eat them greedily all the same, because they were oranges.

He turned up the velvet collar of his overcoat. He did not look at anybody. He knew that he had to turn left and that the grave he was looking for was the third after the cypresses.

All around, flowers had been placed on the graves. The day before, women had washed some of the tombstones with soap and water. The railings had been re-painted.

'Excuse me! No smoking ...'

The chief-inspector scarcely realized that he was being spoken to. Finally he stared at the bell-ringer, who was also the graveyard keeper, and thrust his lighted pipe into his pocket.

He could not manage to think about one thing at a time. Memories flooded in on him, memories of his father, of a friend who had been drowned in the Notre-Dame pond, and the child of the château in his handsome baby-carriage ...

People looked at him. He looked at them. He had already seen those faces. But then, that man who had a child in his arms, for example, and was accompanied by a pregnant woman, had been a kid of four or five ...

Maigret had no flowers. The tombstone was dirty. He walked out of the graveyard in a bad temper, making a whole group turn round as he muttered:

'The first thing we must do is to find the missal!'

He did not feel like returning to the château. Something there distressed him, made him indignant even.

Admittedly he had no illusions about humanity But he was furious that his childhood memories should have been sullied. The countess above all, whom he had always seen as a noble, beautiful person like a picture-book heroine ...

And now she turned out to be a crazy old woman who kept a succession of gigolos.

Not even that. It wasn't frank and open. The notorious Jean pretended to be her secretary. He was not handsome, and not very young either.

And the poor old woman, as her son said, was torn between the château and the church.

And the last Comte de Saint-Fiacre was going to be arrested for signing a bad cheque.

*

Somebody was walking in front of Maigret with his gun on his shoulder, and the chief-inspector suddenly realized that he was making towards the steward's house. He thought he could recognize the figure he had seen from a distance in the fields.

A few feet separated the two men when they reached the yard where some hens were nestling against a wall, sheltering from the wind, with their feathers quivering.

'Hey!'

The man with the gun turned round.

'You're the Saint-Fiacres' steward, aren't you?'

'And who are you?'

'Chief-Inspector Maigret, from Police Headquarters.'

'Maigret?'

The steward was struck by the name, but could not manage to place it.

'You've heard the news?'

'I've just been told ... I was out shooting ... What are the police ...?'

He was a short, sturdy, grey-haired man with a skin furrowed with fine, deep wrinkles, and eyes which looked as if they were lying in ambush behind thick brows.

'They told me that her heart ...'

'Where are you going?'

'Well, I can't go into the château with my boots caked with mud and my gun ...'

A rabbit's head was hanging from the game bag. Maigret looked at the house towards which they were walking.

'Well, well! They've changed the kitchen ...'

A suspicious gaze was fixed on him.

'A good fifteen years ago,' growled the steward.

'What's your name?'

'Gautier ... Is it true that Monsieur le Comte arrived without ...'

32

All this was hesitant, reticent. And Gautier did not ask Maigret to come in. He pushed open the door.

The chief-inspector walked in all the same and turned right towards the dining-room, which smelt of biscuits and old brandy.

'Come in here for a moment, Monsieur Gautier ... They don't need you over there ... And I've a few questions to ask you ...'

'Hurry up!' said a woman's voice in the kitchen. 'They say it's awful ...'

Maigret felt the oak table with the corners decorated with carved lions. It was the same table as in his time. It had been sold to the new steward when his father had died.

'You'll have something to drink, won't you?'

Gautier took a bottle out of the sideboard, perhaps to save time.

'What do you think of that Monsieur Jean? ... Now I come to think of it, what's his surname?'

'Métayer ... Quite a good Bourges family ...'

'Did he cost the countess a lot?'

Gautier filled the glasses with brandy but maintained a stubborn silence.

'What had he got to do at the château? As steward, I suppose you look after everything ...'

'Everything!'

'Well?'

'He didn't do anything ... A few personal letters ... In the beginning he claimed to be able to make money for Madame la Comtesse, thanks to his financial knowledge ... He bought some shares which dropped in value in a few months ... He maintained that he'd win everything back thanks to a new photographic process one of his friends had invented ... That cost Madame la Comtesse about a hundred thousand francs, and the friend disappeared ... Finally the latest thing was some business of printing negatives ... I don't know anything about it ... Something like photogravure, or heliogravure, but cheaper ...'

'Jean Métayer was very busy, in fact ...'

'He bustled about a lot for nothing ... He wrote some articles for the *Journal de Moulins* and they were forced to accept them because of Madame la Comtesse ... It was there that he tried out his negatives and the editor didn't dare throw him out ... Good health!'

Suddenly anxious, he asked:

'Nothing happened between him and Monsieur le Comte?'

'Nothing at all.'

'I suppose it's just a coincidence you being here ... There's no reason why you should be, seeing it was a case of heart disease ...'

The trouble was that it was impossible to meet the steward's eyes. He wiped his moustache and went into the next room.

'Will you excuse me while I change? ... I was going to go to High Mass and now ...'

'I'll see you later,' said Maigret as he left.

And he had no sooner shut the door than he heard the woman who had remained invisible ask:

'Who was that?'

They had laid paving-stones in the yard where he used to play marbles on the beaten earth.

*

The square was full of groups of people in their Sunday best, and organ music was coming from the church. The children, in their new clothes, did not dare to play. And everywhere handkerchiefs were being brought out of pockets, and red noses were being blown noisily.

Snatches of conversation reached Maigret's ears:

'He's a policeman from Paris ...'

'They say he's come about the cow that died last week at Mathieu's ...'

A young man all dressed up in a navy-blue suit with a red flower in his button-hole, his face well scrubbed, his hair shining with brilliantine, ventured to say to the chief-inspector:

'They're waiting for you at Tatin's about the lad who stole ...'

And he nudged his companions, holding back a laugh which burst out all the same while he turned his head away.

He was telling the truth. At Marie Tatin's the atmosphere was now warmer and thicker. Pipes and pipes of tobacco had been smoked. A family of peasants, at one table, were eating food they had brought from the farm, and drinking large bowls of coffee. The father was cutting a dried sausage with his pocket-knife.

The young men were drinking lemonade, and the old men brandy. And Marie Tatin kept trotting around without stopping.

In one corner a woman stood up when the chief-inspector came in, and took a step towards him, worried, hesitant, moist-lipped. She had one hand on the shoulder of a little boy whose red hair Maigret recognized.

'Are you the chief-inspector?'

Everybody looked in her direction.

'First of all, Chief-Inspector, I want to tell you our family has always been honest ... We're poor all the same ... You understand? ... When I saw that Ernest ...'

The boy, very pale-faced, stared straight ahead, without showing the slightest emotion.

'Was it you who took the missal?' asked Maigret, bending down.

No reply. A wild, piercing look.

'Answer the chief-inspector ...'

35

But the lad did not open his mouth. It happened in a
flash. The mother gave him a slap which left a red mark
on his left cheek. The boy's head shook for a moment.
The eyes became a little more moist, the lips trembled,
but he did not budge.

'Are you going to answer, curse of my life?'

And to Maigret she said:

'There's today's kids for you! ... He's been crying for
months to get me to buy him a missal. A thick one like
Monsieur le Curé's! Have you ever heard the like? ...
So, when I heard about Madame la Comtesse's missal, I
thought straight away ... Besides, I was surprised to
see him come home between the second Mass and the
third, because usually he eats at the presbytery ... I went
up to his room and I found this under the mattress ...'

Once again the mother's hand descended on the boy's
cheek. He made no attempt to ward off the blow.

'When I was his age, I couldn't even read. But I'd never
have had enough wickedness in me to steal a book ...'

There was a respectful silence in the inn. Maigret had
the missal in his hands.

'Thank you, Madame ...'

He was in a hurry to examine it. He made as if to
walk to the far end of the room.

'Chief-Inspector ...'

The woman was calling him back. She looked embarrassed.

'They told me there was a reward ... It isn't because
Ernest ...'

Maigret handed her twenty francs which she put carefully away in her bag. After which she pulled her son
towards the door, grumbling:

'As for you, you jail-bird, you just wait ...'

Maigret's eyes met the boy's. It was a matter of only
a few seconds. All the same, they both understood that
they were friends.

Perhaps because Maigret, in his childhood, had longed for – without ever possessing one – a gilt-edged missal with not only the Ordinary of the Mass, but all the liturgical texts in two columns, in Latin and French.

*

'What time will you be coming back to lunch?'

'I don't know.'

Maigret nearly went up to his room to examine the missal, but the memory of the countless draughts which the roof let in made him choose the main road.

It was while walking slowly towards the château that he opened the book, whose binding was embossed with the Saint-Fiacre coat of arms. Or rather he did not open it. The missal opened itself at a page where a piece of paper had been inserted between two leaves.

Page 221. *Prayers After Communion*.

What was there was a piece of newspaper cut out anyhow which immediately struck the eye as most peculiar, as if it had been badly printed.

Paris, 1 November. A dramatic suicide took place this morning in a flat in the Rue de Miromesnil which had been occupied for several years by the Comte de Saint-Fiacre and his mistress, a Russian woman called Marie S ...

After telling his mistress that he was ashamed of the scandalous conduct of a certain member of his family, the count fired a bullet into his head and died a few minutes later without recovering consciousness.

We understand that a distressing family drama lies behind this incident and that the person mentioned above is none other than the dead man's mother.

A goose wandering on to the road stretched out towards Maigret a beak wide open in fury. The bells were in full peal and the congregation was shuffling slowly out of the little church, from which smells of incense and extinguished tapers were escaping.

Maigret had thrust the bulky missal into his overcoat pocket, where it made a bulge. He had stopped to examine the fateful scrap of paper.

The murder weapon! A newspaper cutting two inches by three!

The Comtesse de Saint-Fiacre went to the first Mass, and knelt down in the stall which for two centuries had been reserved for members of her family.

And here was the weapon! Maigret turned the piece of paper over and over. There was something peculiar about it. Among other things he noticed the alignment of the type and felt sure that the printing had not been done on a rotary press, as in the case of a real newspaper.

This was just a proof, pulled by hand. That was obvious from the fact that the other side of the piece of paper bore exactly the same text.

The murderer had not taken the trouble to produce a finished piece of work, or else he had not had enough time. Besides, would the countess be likely to think of turning the piece of paper over? Wouldn't she have died first from shock, indignation, shame and fear?

The expression on Maigret's face was terrifying, because he had never before encountered a crime which was so cowardly and so clever at the same time.

And the murderer had had the nerve to warn the police!

Supposing that the missal had not been found . . .

Yes, that was it! The missal was not intended to be found! For then it was impossible to talk about a crime, or to accuse anybody. The countess had died from heart failure.

He turned back suddenly. He arrived at Marie Tatin's when everybody was talking about him and the missal.

'You know where little Ernest lives?'

'The third house after the grocer's, in the High Street . . .'

He hurried round there. It was a small single-story house. There were photographs of the father and mother on the wall, on either side of the sideboard. The woman, who had already changed out of her Sunday best, was in the kitchen, which smelt of roast beef.

'Isn't your son here?'

'He's changing. There's no point in him getting his best clothes dirty . . . You saw what a scolding I gave him! . . . A child who has nothing but good examples in front of him and . . .'

She opened the door and shouted:

'Come here, you bad lot!'

He caught sight of the boy in his underpants, trying to hide.

'Let him get dressed,' said Maigret. 'I'll talk to him later . . .'

The woman went on preparing the lunch. Her husband was presumably at Marie Tatin's, having his apéritif.

At last the door opened and Ernest came in, with a sly look on his face, wearing his weekday suit, the trousers of which were too long.

'You want him to go out with you?' exclaimed the woman. 'But in that case . . . Ernest . . . Go and put your best suit on quick . . .'

'It isn't worth it, Madame . . . Come along, lad . . .'

The street was empty. All the life of the district was concentrated in the square, in the graveyard, and at Marie Tatin's.

'Tomorrow I'm going to give you an even thicker missal, with the first letter of every word in red . . .'

The boy was dumbfounded. So the chief-inspector knew that there were missals with red letters, like the one on the altar?

'Only, you're going to tell me frankly where you found this one. I shan't scold you ...'

It was strange to see the old peasant mistrust awakening in the boy. He said nothing. He was already on the defensive.

'Was it on the prayer-stool that you found it?'

Silence. There were freckles on his cheeks and the bridge of his nose. His thick lips were trying to keep still.

'Don't you understand that I'm your friend?'

'Yes ... You gave Ma twenty francs ...'

'Well, what of it?'

The child took his revenge.

'When we got back home Ma told me she'd only slapped me for show, and she gave me fifty centimes ...'

The boy knew what he was doing all right. What was going on inside that head of his which was too big for his thin body?

'And what about the sacristan?'

'He didn't say anything to me ...'

'Who took the missal from the prayer-stool?'

'I don't know ...'

'Where did you find it?'

'Under my surplice, in the sacristy ... I was supposed to go and have breakfast in the presbytery. I'd forgotten my handkerchief ... When I moved my surplice, I felt something hard ...'

'Was the sacristan there?'

'He was in the church, putting out the candles ... You know, a missal with red letters costs an awful lot ...'

In other words, somebody had taken the missal from the prayerstool and had hidden it for the time being in the sacristy, under the choirboy's surplice, obviously with the intention of coming back for it later.

'Did you open it?'

'I didn't have time ... I wanted my boiled egg ... Because on Sunday ...'

'I know ...'

And Ernest wondered how this man from the town could possibly know that on Sunday he had an egg and some bread and jam at the presbytery.

'You can go ...'

'Is it true that I'll have ...?'

'A missal, yes ... Tomorrow .. Goodbye, lad ...'

Maigret held out his hand and after a moment's hesitation the boy gave him his.

'I know you're just joking,' he said, however, as he went off.

A crime in three stages: somebody had set the article, or had it set, with a linotype, which could only be found in a newspaper building or a big printing-house.

Somebody had slipped the piece of paper into the missal, after choosing the page.

And somebody had collected the missal and hidden it temporarily under the surplice in the sacristy.

Perhaps the same man had done everything. Perhaps each operation had been carried out by a different person. Or perhaps the same person had been responsible for two of the three operations.

As he was passing in front of the church, Maigret saw the priest coming out and walking towards him. He waited for him under the poplars, near the woman selling oranges and chocolate.

'I'm going to the château,' he said as he joined the chief-inspector. 'That's the first time I've celebrated Mass without even knowing what I was doing ... The idea that a crime ...'

'It was a crime all right,' said Maigret laconically.

They walked along in silence. Without saying a word, the chief-inspector held out the scrap of paper to his companion, who read it and handed it back.

And they walked another hundred yards without speaking.

'One evil leads to another ... But she was a poor creature ...'

They both had to hold on to their hats because of the wind, which was increasing in violence.

'I wasn't strict enough,' the priest added in a gloomy voice.

'You?'

'Every day she would come back to me ... She was ready to return to the ways of the Lord ... But every day, over there ...'

There was a bitter note in his voice.

'I refused to go there and yet it was my duty ...'

They nearly stopped, because two men were walking along the main drive of the château and they were bound to meet them. They recognized the doctor, with his little brown beard, and beside him, the tall thin figure of Jean Métayer who was still talking excitedly. The yellow car was in the courtyard. Maigret guessed that Métayer did not dare go back to the château as long as the Comte de Saint-Fiacre was there.

There was an ambiguous light over the village. The situation was ambiguous too, with all these vague comings and goings.

'Come along!' said Maigret.

The doctor must have said the same thing to the secretary, whom he brought along with him. When he was near enough he said:

'Good morning, Monsieur le Curé! You know, I'm in a position to reassure you ... Sinner though I am, I can imagine your distress at the idea that a crime may have been committed in your church ... Well, no . . Science is categorical...*Our* countess died from heart failure...'

Maigret had gone up to Jean Métayer.

'I'd like to ask you a question ...'

He could feel that the young man was on edge, panting with fear.

'When did you last go to the *Journal de Moulins*?'

'I ... Wait a minute ...'

He was about to speak. But his suspicions were aroused. He darted a distrustful look at the chief-inspector.

'Why do you ask me that?'

'It doesn't matter.'

'Am I obliged to reply?'

'You are free to say nothing.'

Perhaps not exactly the face of a degenerate, but an anxious, tormented face. And a quite exceptional nervousness, capable of interesting Doctor Bouchardon, who was talking to the priest.

'I know that I'm the one who's going to suffer! ... But I'm not going to take it lying down ...'

'Of course you're not going to take it lying down ...'

'First I want to see a lawyer ... I'm entitled to that ... Besides, by what right are you ...?'

'Just a minute! Have you ever studied law?'

'For two years.'

He was trying to regain his composure, to smile.

'Nobody has laid a charge, and nobody has been caught in *flagrante delicto* ... So you've no right to ...'

'Very good! Ten out of ten!'

'The doctor says ...'

'And I maintain that the countess was killed by the dirtiest swine imaginable. Read this!'

And Maigret held out the printed piece of paper to him. Stiffening suddenly, Jean Métayer looked at him as if he were going to spit in his face.

'A ... You said a ...? I won't stand for ...'

The chief-inspector, gently putting his hand on his shoulder, said:

'But my poor boy, I haven't said anything yet, *to you*. Where's the count? Read that all the same. You can give it back to me later ...'

A gleam of triumph shone in Métayer's eyes.

'The count is discussing cheques with the steward ... You'll find them in the library ...'

The priest and the doctor were walking in front and Maigret heard the doctor's voice saying:

'Certainly not, Monsieur le Curé. It's human! Terribly human! If only you'd studied a little physiology instead of poring over the writings of Saint Augustine ...'

And the gravel crunched under the feet of the four men who slowly climbed the steps, which the cold had made whiter and harder than ever.

4 Marie Vassilief

Maigret could not be everywhere. The château was huge.
That was why he had only a vague idea of the morning's
events.

It was the time when, on Sundays and holidays, the
peasants put off the moment of going home, savouring
the pleasure of being in a well-dressed group in the
village square or else in a café. Some were already drunk.
Others were talking in loud voices. And the children in
their stiff clothes were looking admiringly at their daddies.

Inside the château, Jean Métayer, looking rather
yellow in the face, had gone upstairs, all alone, to the
first floor, where he could be heard walking up and down
one room.

'If you'll come with me,' the doctor said to the priest.
And he lured him away in the direction of the dead
woman's bedroom.

On the ground floor, a wide corridor ran the entire
length of the building, lined by a row of doors. Maigret
could hear a hum of voices. He had been told that the
Comte de Saint-Fiacre and the steward were in the
library.

He decided to go in there, opened the wrong door,
and found himself in the drawing-room. The communi-
cating-door leading into the library was open. In a gilt-
edged mirror he caught sight of the reflection of the
young man sitting on one corner of the desk, looking
utterly depressed, and that of the steward, solidly planted
on his stocky legs.

'You ought to have known that there was no point in insisting,' Gautier was saying. 'Especially for forty thousand francs!'

'Who answered the telephone when I called?'

'Monsieur Jean, of course.'

'So that he didn't even pass on the message to my mother?'

Maigret coughed and walked into the library.

'What telephone call are you talking about?'

Maurice de Saint-Fiacre answered without any embarrassment:

'The one I made the day before yesterday to the château. As I've already told you, I needed some money. I wanted to ask my mother for the required sum. But it was that . . . that Monsieur Jean, as they call him here, who answered the telephone . . .'

'And he told you that there was nothing doing? You came here all the same . . .'

The steward was watching the two men. Maurice had left the desk on which he had been perched.

'In any case, I didn't bring Gautier here to talk about that,' he said irritably. 'I haven't concealed the situation from you, Chief-Inspector. Tomorrow a charge will be laid against me. It's obvious that with my mother dead, I'm the only natural heir. I therefore asked Gautier to get me forty thousand francs for tomorrow morning . . . Well, it seems that that's impossible . . .'

'Quite impossible!' repeated the steward.

'Apparently nothing can be done without the permission of the lawyer, who won't gather the interested parties together until after the funeral. And Gautier adds that, quite apart from that, it would be difficult to raise a loan of forty thousand francs on the property which remains . . .'

He started walking up and down.

'It's clear, isn't it? All cut and dried! I may even be

prevented from attending the funeral ... But now I come to think of it ... One more question ... You spoke of a crime ... Is it ...?'

'No charge has been laid, and probably no charge will be laid,' said Maigret. 'So the case won't come up before the courts ...'

'Leave us alone, Gautier.'

As soon as the steward had reluctantly left the room, he went on:

'A crime, really?'

'A crime which doesn't concern the police.'

'Explain yourself ... I'm beginning to ...'

But just then they heard a woman's voice in the hall, accompanied by the deeper voice of the steward. Maurice frowned and made for the door, which he pulled open with an abrupt gesture.

'Marie! What the ...?'

'Maurice! Why won't they let me in? ... It's insufferable! I've been waiting for an hour at the hotel ...'

She spoke with a pronounced foreign accent. It was Marie Vassilief, who had arrived from Moulins in an old taxi which they could see in the courtyard.

She was tall and very beautiful, with hair which was perhaps artificially fair. Seeing that Maigret was looking at her closely, she started talking volubly in English, and Maurice answered her in the same language.

She asked him if he had any money. He replied that there was no longer any question of that, that his mother was dead, and that she must go back to Paris, where he would join her soon.

At this she asked with a laugh:

'What shall I use for money? I haven't even enough to pay for the taxi!'

Maurice de Saint-Fiacre began to panic. His mistress's shrill voice rang through the château and lent a scandalous quality to the scene.

The steward was still in the corridor.

'If you stay here, I'm staying with you!' declared Marie Vassilief.

Maigret told Gautier:

'Pay the taxi-driver and send him away.'

The confusion was growing. Not a material, reparable confusion, but a moral confusion which seemed to be contagious. Gautier himself was losing his composure.

'I must have a word with you, Chief-Inspector,' the young man said.

'Not now.'

And he gestured towards the aggressively elegant woman who was walking around the library and drawing-room as if she were compiling an inventory.

'Who is this silly portrait of, Maurice?' she exclaimed with a laugh.

There were footsteps on the stairs. Maigret saw Métayer go past, wearing a loose-fitting overcoat and carrying a travelling-bag. Métayer must have guessed that he would not be allowed to leave, for he stopped outside the library door and waited.

'Where are you going?'

'To the inn ... It's more fitting that I should ...'

To get rid of his mistress, Maurice de Saint-Fiacre took her off towards the right wing of the château. The two went on talking in English.

'Is it true that it would be impossible to raise a loan of forty thousand francs on the château?' Maigret asked the steward.

'It would be difficult.'

'Well, do it all the same, by tomorrow morning at the latest.'

The chief-inspector was reluctant to go out. At the last moment he decided to go up to the first floor and there a surprise was waiting for him. While downstairs everybody was bustling about aimlessly, order had been restored in the Comtesse de Saint-Fiacre's bedroom.

It was no longer the ambiguous, sordid atmosphere of that morning. It was no longer even the same body. The dead woman, clothed in a white nightdress, was stretched out on her four-poster bed in a peaceful, dignified attitude, with her hands folded on a crucifix.

Already there were lighted tapers, some holy water, and a sprig of boxwood in a bowl.

Bouchardon looked at Maigret as he came in and seemed to be saying:

'Well, what do you think about it? Nice work, isn't it?'

The priest was praying, moving his lips silently. He remained alone with the dead woman while the other two went off.

The groups in the square had thinned out in front of the church. Through the curtains in the house windows, families could be seen sitting at lunch.

For a few seconds, the sun tried to penetrate the layer of clouds, but only the next moment the sky turned grey again and the trees trembled more than ever.

Jean Métayer was installed in the corner near the window and he was eating automatically while looking at the empty road. Maigret had taken his seat at the other end of the inn room. Between the two of them there was a family from a neighbouring village who had arrived in a lorry. They had brought their own food and Marie Tatin was serving them with drinks.

The poor Tatin woman was distraught. She could no longer make head or tail of what was happening. Usually she only let an attic room from time to time to a workman who came to carry out repairs at the château or on a farm.

And now, besides Maigret, she had a new guest: the countess's secretary.

She did not dare to ask any questions. All morning she

had heard frightening stories told by her customers. Among other things she had heard mention of the police ...

'I'm very much afraid the chicken is overcooked,' she said as she served Maigret.

The tone of voice was the same in which she would have said, for example:

'I'm afraid of everything! I don't know what's happening! Mother of God, protect me!'

The chief-inspector gazed at her tenderly. She had always had this same timid, sickly look.

'Do you remember, Marie, the ...'

She opened her eyes wide. She was already beginning a defensive movement.

'... the business of the frogs?'

'But ... Who ...?'

'Your mother had sent you to pick mushrooms in the meadow behind the Notre-Dame pond ... There were three little boys playing over there ... They took advantage of a moment when you were thinking of something else to replace the mushrooms in the basket with frogs ... And all the way home you were frightened because things were moving about ...'

For a few moments she had been looking at him closely and she ended up by stammering:

'Maigret?'

'Careful! Monsieur Jean has finished his chicken and is waiting for the next course.'

And now Marie Tatin had changed. She was even more agitated than before, but with moments of confidence.

How funny life was! Years and years without the slightest incident, without anything happening to relieve the daily monotony. And then, all of a sudden, incomprehensible events, dramatic happenings, things such as you did not even read about in the papers!

Now and then, while waiting on Jean Métayer and the peasants, she darted a conspiratorial glance at Maigret. When he had finished, she said shyly:

'You'll have a glass of brandy, won't you?'

'You used to say *tu* in the old days, Marie!'

She laughed. No, she did not dare to any more.

'But *you* haven't had any lunch!'

'Yes, I have! I never stop eating in the kitchen . . . A mouthful now . . . A mouthful later . . .'

A motor-cycle went by along the road. Maigret caught a glimpse of a young man who looked smarter than most of the inhabitants of Saint-Fiacre.

'Who's that?'

'Didn't you see him this morning? It's Emile Gautier, the steward's son.'

'Where is he going?'

'Probably to Moulins . . . He's practically a townsman. He works in a bank . . .'

People could be seen coming out of their houses, walking along the road, or making for the graveyard.

Curiously enough, Maigret was sleepy. He felt harassed, as if he had made an exceptional effort. And this was not because he had got up at half past five in the morning, nor because he had caught cold.

It was rather the atmosphere which was crushing him. He felt personally affected by the drama, disgusted by it.

Yes, disgusted. That was the word for it. He had never imagined that he would find his native village in these circumstances. Down to his father's grave, on which the tombstone had turned black, and where somebody had forbidden him to smoke! Opposite him, Jean Métayer was putting on a show. He knew that he was being watched. He was trying to keep calm while he was eating, and even to put on a vaguely contemptuous smile.

'A glass of brandy?' Marie Tatin asked him too.

'No, thank you. I never touch spirits.'

He was well-bred. He made a point of displaying his good manners at every opportunity. At the inn, he ate with the same affected gestures as at the château.

When he had finished his lunch, he asked:

'Have you a telephone?'

'No, but there's a call-box over the way ...'

He crossed the road, and went on to the grocer's shop run by the sacristan, where the call-box was installed. He must have asked for a long-distance call, for Maigret saw him waiting a long time in the shop, smoking one cigarette after another.

When he returned, the peasants had left the inn. Marie Tatin was washing the glasses in readiness for Vespers which would bring more customers.

'To whom have you just telephoned? Remember that I can find out by asking the operator ...'

'To my father in Bourges.'

His voice was curt, aggressive.

'I asked him to send me a lawyer straight away.'

He made Maigret think of a ridiculous little mongrel which bares its teeth before anyone even makes as if to touch it.

'You seem very sure of being bothered?'

'I must ask you not to speak to me again until my lawyer gets here. You can believe me when I say I'm sorry there's only one inn in this village.'

Did he hear the word the chief-inspector muttered as he walked away?

'Cretin! ... Dirty little cretin!'

And Marie Tatin, without knowing why, felt frightened of remaining alone with him.

*

The day was to continue to the very end to be marked by confusion and indecision, probably because nobody felt qualified to take command of events.

Maigret, wrapped up in his heavy overcoat, roamed around the village. At one time he was seen in the square in front of the church, at another in the vicinity of the château, where the windows lit up one after another.

For night was falling fast. The church was brightly lit, vibrating with the sound of the organ. The bell-ringer locked the graveyard gate.

And groups of people who were scarcely visible in the darkness consulted one another. They did not know whether or not to call at the château to pay their respects to the dead woman. Two men went off to see, and were received by the butler, who did not know what to do either. There was no tray ready for the visiting cards of callers. The servant went to look for Maurice de Saint-Fiacre to ask his opinion, but the Russian woman replied that he had gone out for a breath of air.

She for her part was lying on her bed, fully dressed, and smoking cigarettes with cardboard tips

So the butler shrugged his shoulders and let the two callers in.

This was taken as a signal. After Vespers, there were consultations.

'Yes, I tell you! Old Martin and young Bonnet have already been!'

Everybody went in a procession. The château was poorly lit. The peasants walked along the corridor, silhouetted in turn against each window. They pulled their children along by the hand, shaking them to stop them from making any noise. The stairs ... The first floor corridor ... And finally the bedroom where these people had never set foot before.

There was nobody there but the countess's chamber-maid, who watched the invasion in alarm. The peasants made the sign of the cross with a sprig of boxwood dipped in the holy water. The bolder spirits murmured in an undertone:

53

'You'd think she was asleep!'

And others echoed them:

'She didn't suffer . . .'

Then their footsteps sounded on the disjointed floor. The stairs creaked. There were murmurs of:

'Hush! . . . Hold the banisters tight . . .'

The cook, in her basement kitchen, could see only the legs of the people passing by.

Maurice de Saint-Fiacre came back while the house was still full of people. He looked at the peasants in wide-eyed surprise. The callers wondered if they ought to speak to him. But he just muttered at them and went into Marie Vassilief's bedroom where he could be heard talking in English.

Maigret, for his part, was in the church. The sacristan, holding the candle-extinguisher, was going from taper to taper. The priest was taking off his vestments in the sacristy.

On both left and right were the confessionals with their little green curtains intended to conceal the penitents. Maigret remembered the time when his face had not reached high enough to be hidden by the curtain.

Behind him, the bell-ringer, who had not seen him, was bolting the main door.

The chief-inspector suddenly crossed the nave and went into the sacristy where the priest was surprised to see him appear unexpectedly.

'Excuse me, Monsieur le Curé . . . Before anything else, I would like to ask you a question . . .'

In front of him, the priest's regular features wore a solemn expression, but it seemed to Maigret that his eyes were shining feverishly.

'This morning, something strange occurred here. The countess's missal, which was on her prayer-stool, suddenly disappeared and was later found hidden under the choirboy's surplice, in this very room . . .'

54

Silence. The sound of the sacristan's footsteps on the carpet in the church. The heavier footsteps of the bell-ringer who was leaving through a side door.

'Only four people could have done that ... Please forgive me ... The choirboy, the sacristan, the bell-ringer ...'

'And I!'

The voice was calm. The priest's face was lit on only one side by the flickering flame of a candle. From a censer a thin wisp of blue smoke was spiralling up towards the ceiling.

'It was ...?'

'It was I who took the missal and put it here, until such time ...'

The ciborium, the altar-cruets, and the sanctus bell were in their places as in the days when little Maigret had been a choirboy.

'Did you know what was inside the missal?'

'No.'

'In that case ...'

'I must ask you not to put any more questions to me, Monsieur Maigret. I am under the seal of the confessional ...'

By an involuntary association of ideas, the chief-inspector remembered his catechism. He also remembered the scene he had pictured when the old Curé had told the story of a priest in the Middle Ages who had allowed his tongue to be torn out rather than break the seal of the confessional. He saw it again in every detail in his mind's eye, after thirty-five years.

'You know who the murderer is,' he murmured all the same.

'God knows who he is ... Excuse me ... I have to go and see a sick person ...'

They went out through the presbytery garden. A little gate separated it from the road. Over there, some people who had come from the château were standing about in groups, a little way off, and discussing what had happened.

'You don't think, Monsieur le Curé, that it's your place to . . .'

But they bumped into the doctor, who muttered under his breath:

'I say, Curé, don't you think the place is turning into something of a bawdy-house? . . . Somebody ought to try to clean it up, if only to safeguard the peasants' morals! . . . Oh, so you're here, too, Chief-Inspector! Well, you've done some good work, I must say . . . At the moment, half the village is accusing the young count of . . . Especially since that woman arrived! . . . The steward is going to see the farmers to collect the forty thousand francs which, so it seems, are needed to . . .'

'Oh, go to blazes!'

Maigret walked away. He felt sick at heart. And now he was being accused of being the cause of all this trouble. What blunder had he committed? Indeed, what had he done? He would have given anything to see the situation develop in a dignified atmosphere.

He strode along towards the inn which was half full. He caught only one phrase:

'They say that if he can't find the money, he'll go to prison . . .'

Marie Tatin was the picture of misery. She came and went, a brisk little figure, trotting along like an old woman, although she was not more than forty.

'Is the lemonade for you? . . . Who ordered two beers?'

In his corner, Jean Métayer was writing, raising his head now and then to listen to the conversations.

Maigret went over to him. He could not read the cramped handwriting, but he saw that the paragraphs were clearly divided, with only a few corrections, and each one preceded by a number.

56

1 ...
2 ...
3 ...

The secretary was preparing his defence, while waiting for his lawyer to arrive ...

A few feet away, a woman was saying:

'There weren't any clean sheets and they had to go and borrow some from the steward's wife.'

Pale, with drawn features, but a determined look in his eyes, Jean Métayer wrote down:

4 ...

5 The Second Day

Maigret slept that restless yet voluptuous sleep which you experience only in a cold country bedroom which smells of the cowshed, winter apples and hay. Draughts were blowing all around him. And the sheets were icy, except in the one spot, a soft, cosy hollow, which he had warmed with his body. So that, rolled up in a ball, he avoided making the slightest movement.

Several times, he had heard Jean Métayer's dry cough in the next room. Then came the furtive footsteps of Marie Tatin getting up.

He stayed in bed a few minutes longer. When he had lighted the candle, he had not the courage to wash with the icy water in the jug, and he put off that operation until later, going down in his slippers, without a collar.

Downstairs, Marie Tatin was pouring paraffin on the fire, which was refusing to take. She had her hair in curlers and she blushed as she saw the chief-inspector come in.

'It isn't seven o'clock yet ... The coffee isn't ready ...'

Maigret had a slight worry. Half an hour earlier, when he had been half asleep, he had thought he heard a car driving past. Now, Saint-Fiacre is not on the main road. Almost the only traffic is the bus which goes through the village once a day.

'The bus hasn't gone, has it, Marie?'

'Never before half past eight! And more often than not, nine o'clock ...'

'Is that the bell for Mass ringing already?'

'Yes ... It's at seven o'clock in the winter, and six o'clock in summer ... If you want to warm yourself ...'

She pointed to the fire which was finally burning up.

'You really can't bring yourself to call me *tu*?'

Maigret could have bitten his tongue off as he saw a coquettish smile appear on the poor woman's face.

'The coffee will be ready in five minutes ...'

It would not be light before eight o'clock. The cold was even sharper than the day before. With his coat collar turned up, and his hat pulled down over his eyes, Maigret walked slowly towards the bright patch of the church.

It was no longer a Holy Day. There were no more than three women in the nave. And the Mass had something scamped and furtive about it. The priest went too quickly from one corner of the altar to another. He turned round too quickly too, with his arms outstretched to mumble:

Dominus vobiscum!

The choirboy, who was having some difficulty in following him, said: *Amen* at the wrong time.

Was the panic going to set in again? He could hear the murmur of the liturgical prayers and now and then a gasp from the priest as he got his breath back between two words.

Ite missa est ...

Had this particular Mass lasted as much as twelve minutes? The three women stood up. The priest was reciting the last Gospel. A car drew up in front of the church and soon hesitant footsteps could be heard outside.

Maigret had remained at the back of the nave, standing right against the door. Consequently, when the door opened, the new arrival found himself literally face to face with the chief-inspector.

It was Maurice de Saint-Fiacre. He was so surprised that he nearly beat a retreat, murmuring:

'I beg your pardon ... I ...'

But he took a step forward, and made an effort to regain his composure.

'Is Mass over?'

His nerves were obviously on edge. There were rings under his eyes as if he had not slept a wink all night. And by opening the door, he had brought the cold air in with him.

'Have you come from Moulins?'

The two men were talking with forced politeness while the priest was reciting the prayer after the Gospel and the women were shutting their missals and picking up their handbags and umbrellas.

'How did you know? Yes ... I ...'

'Shall we go out?'

The priest and the choirboy had gone into the sacristy and the sacristan was putting out the two tapers which had been sufficient for the Low Mass.

Outside, the sky was a little lighter along the horizon. The white walls of the nearest houses stood out in the half-light. The yellow car was there, between the trees in the square.

Saint-Fiacre's embarrassment was obvious. He looked at Maigret in some surprise, astonished perhaps at seeing him unshaven, without a collar under his coat.

'You got up early!' murmured the chief-inspector.

'The first train, which is an express, leaves Moulins at three minutes past seven ...'

'I don't understand ... You didn't take the train, seeing that ...'

'You're forgetting Marie Vassilief ...'

It was all so simple. And so natural. The presence of Maurice's mistress could only be an embarrassment at the château. So he had driven her to Moulins, put her on the train for Paris, and on his way back had dropped into the lighted church.

But Maigret was not satisfied. He was trying to follow the anxious glances of the count, who seemed to be waiting for somebody or to be afraid of something.

'She doesn't look an easy person to deal with!' hinted the chief-inspector.

'She's known better days. So she's very sensitive ... The idea that I might want to hide our liaison ...'

'Which has been going on for how long?'

'Just under a year ... Marie doesn't care about money ... There have been difficult times ...'

His gaze had at last settled on one point. Maigret followed it and caught sight of the priest who had just come out of the church behind him. He had the impression that the two gazes met and that the priest was as embarrassed as the Comte de Saint-Fiacre.

The chief-inspector was going to call to him. But already, with clumsy haste, the priest called out a rather curt greeting to the two men and went into the presbytery as if he were running away.

'He doesn't look like a country priest ...'

Maurice made no reply. Through the lighted window they could see the priest sitting down to his breakfast, and the housekeeper bringing him a steaming coffee-pot.

Some little boys with satchels on their backs were beginning to make their way to school. The surface of the Notre-Dame pond was turning the colour of a mirror.

'What arrangements have you made for ...' began Maigret.

And the other broke in far too quickly:

'For what?'

'For the funeral ... Did anybody watch the body last night?'

'No. The idea was mooted for a moment. Gautier said that it wasn't done any more ...'

They heard the roar of a two-stroke engine in the

courtyard of the château. A few moments later a motor-cycle went by on the road, heading for Moulins. Maigret recognized Gautier's son, whom he had seen the day before. He was wearing a fawn raincoat and a check cap.

Maurice de Saint-Fiacre did not know what attitude to adopt. He did not dare to get back into his car. And he had nothing to say to the chief-inspector.

'Has Gautier found the forty thousand francs?'

'No ... Yes ... I mean ...'

Maigret looked at him inquisitively, surprised to see him so flustered.

'Has he found them, or hasn't he? I got the impression yesterday that he was raising difficulties about it. Because in spite of everything, in spite of all the mort-gages and debts, you'll get much more than that amount ...'

No, Maurice still made no reply. He looked panic-stricken, for no apparent reason. And the next thing he said had no connexion with the previous conversation.

'Tell me frankly, Chief-Inspector ... Do you suspect me?'

'Suspect you of what?'

'You know perfectly well ... I've got to know ...'

'I've no more reason to suspect you than anybody else,' Maigret replied evasively.

His companion leapt upon this statement.

'Thank you ... Well, that's what you must tell people ... You understand? ... Otherwise, my position is im-possible ...'

'What's the bank at which your cheque is going to be presented?'

'The Comptoir d'Escompte ...'

A woman was making for the wash-house, pushing a wheelbarrow containing two laundry baskets. The priest, in his presbytery, was walking up and down, reading his breviary, but the chief-inspector had the impression that he kept darting anxious glances at the two men.

'I'll join you at the château.'

'Now?'

'In a little while . . .'

It was clear that Maurice de Saint-Fiacre did not relish the idea at all. He got into his car like a condemned man. And through the presbytery window the chief-inspector could see the priest watching him drive away.

Maigret wanted to go and put on a collar at the very least. Just as he arrived in front of the inn, Jean Métayer came out of the grocer's. He had simply put a coat on over his pyjamas. He looked at the chief-inspector with a triumphant expression.

'A telephone call?'

The young man retorted acidly:

'My lawyer's arriving at ten to nine.'

He was sure of himself. He sent back some boiled eggs which were under-done, and drummed his fingers on the table.

From the window of his bedroom, where he had gone to get dressed, Maigret could see the courtyard of the château, the sports car, and Maurice de Saint-Fiacre, who did not seem to know what to do. Perhaps he was going to return to the village on foot?

The chief-inspector made haste. A few moments later he for his part was walking towards the château. And the two men met less than a hundred yards from the church.

'Where were you going?' asked Maigret.

'Nowhere. I don't know . . .'

'Perhaps to say your prayers in the church?'

These few words were enough to make his companion turn pale, as if they had a mysterious, terrible meaning.

Maurice de Saint-Fiacre was not made for dramatic events. At first sight he was a tall, strapping fellow, a magnificently healthy sportsman. If you looked more closely, you could see signs of his noble birth. Under the muscles, which were overladen with fat, there was hardly any energy. He had probably just had a sleepless night, and it seemed to have taken all the strength out of him.

'Have you had announcements of the death printed?'

'No.'

'But what about the family ... the local gentry ...?'

The young man lost his temper.

'They wouldn't come! You must know that! Before, yes! When my father was alive ... During the shooting season, there were up to thirty guests at a time at the château for weeks on end ...'

Maigret knew that as well as anybody else, for when there was a shoot, unknown to his parents, he had often put on the white smock of a beater.

'Since then ...'

And Maurice made a gesture which signified:

'Things have gone from bad to worse ...'

The whole of Berry must have talked about the crazy old woman spoiling the last years of her life with her so-called secretaries. And the farms being sold one after another. And the son making a fool of himself in Paris.

'Do you think the funeral can be held tomorrow? ... You understand ... The sooner this situation comes to an end the better ...'

A cart full of manure went slowly by and its big wheels looked as if they were grinding the pebbles on the road. Dawn had broken, a greyer dawn than the day before, but with less wind. From a distance Maigret saw Gautier crossing the courtyard and coming towards him.

Then a strange thing happened.

'Will you excuse me?' the chief-inspector said to his companion, going off in the direction of the château.

He had scarcely gone a hundred yards when he turned round. Maurice de Saint-Fiacre was standing on the doorstep of the presbytery. He must have rung the door-bell. And when he saw that he had been caught out, he walked away quickly without waiting for a reply.

He did not know where to go. His whole bearing showed that he was terribly ill at ease. The chief-inspector reached the steward, who had seen him coming towards him and was waiting for him with an arrogant air.

'What do you want?'

'Just a piece of information. Have you found the forty thousand francs the count needs?'

'No. And I defy anybody to find them round here! Everybody knows just how much his signature is worth.'

'So?'

'So he'll have to manage as best he can. It's none of my business.'

Saint-Fiacre was retracing his steps. Maigret could tell he was longing to take a certain course of action and that for some reason or other that was impossible. Making up his mind, he came towards the château and stopped near the two men.

'Gautier! Come to the library for your instructions.'

He turned to go.

'I'll see you later on, Chief-Inspector,' he added with an effort.

*

When Maigret passed the presbytery, he had a distinct impression of being watched through the curtains. But he could not be sure, for now that the sun had risen, the light inside had been put out.

There was a taxi standing outside Marie Tatin's. Inside the inn, a man of about fifty, immaculately dressed in striped trousers and a black, silk-edged jacket, was sitting at a table with Jean Métayer.

When the chief-inspector came in, he jumped to his feet and rushed forward with outstretched hand.

'I understand that you are an officer from Police Headquarters ... Allow me to introduce myself ... Maître Tallier of the Bourges bar ... Will you have a drink with us?'

Jean Métayer had stood up, but his attitude showed that he did not approve of his lawyer's cordiality.

'Innkeeper! ... Come and take our orders, please ...'

In a conciliatory voice he asked:

'What will you have? ... In this cold weather what do you say to grogs all round? ... Three grogs, my good woman ...'

His good woman was poor Marie Tatin, who was unaccustomed to these ways.

'I hope, Chief-Inspector, that you'll forgive my client ... If I have understood him rightly he has shown a certain mistrust of you ... But don't forget that he's a young man of good family who has nothing on his conscience, and who was revolted by the suspicion he felt all round him ... The bad temper he displayed yesterday, if I may say so, is the best proof of his complete innocence ...'

With Maître Tallier there was no need to open your mouth. He took everything upon himself, questions and replies, accompanying his words with suave gestures.

'Of course, I don't know all the details ... If I have understood correctly, the Comtesse de Saint-Fiacre died yesterday, during the first Mass, from heart failure ... Later, I gather, a piece of paper was found in her missal which suggests that her death was due to a violent shock ... Did the victim's son – who by a coincidence happened to be in the vicinity – lay a charge? ... No! ... In any case, I don't think that a charge would be accepted ... The criminal operation – if it took place – was not sufficiently clear-cut to justify the opening of an official inquiry ...

66

'We are in agreement, are we not? ... No charge, so no legal action ...

'Not that that prevents me from understanding the unofficial inquiries you are carrying out on your own ...

'It isn't enough for my client not to be prosecuted. He must be cleared of all suspicion ...

'Let me make myself clear ... What, after all, was his position at the château? ... That of an adopted son ... The countess, left on her own, parted from a son who caused her nothing but trouble, was comforted by her secretary's devotion and upright character ...

'My client isn't an idler ... He didn't just lead a care-free life as he could have done at the château ... He worked ... He looked for investments ... He even took an interest in recent inventions ...

'Did he stand to benefit in any way from the death of his benefactress? ... Need I say any more? ... I think not ...

'And that, Chief-Inspector, is what I want to help you to establish ...

'I must add that there are a few indispensable measures that I shall have to take in conjunction with the solicitor ... Jean Métayer is a trusting soul ... He never imagined that anything of this sort could happen ...

'His belongings are at the château, mixed up with those of the late countess.

'Now other persons have arrived there who probably intend to lay their hands on ...'

'A few pairs of pyjamas, and some old slippers!' growled Maigret, getting up.

'I beg your pardon?'

During the whole of this conversation Jean Métayer had been taking notes in a little notebook. It was he who calmed down his lawyer, who stood up in his turn.

'Leave it! I realized the very first minute that I had

an enemy in the chief-inspector. And since then I have found that he belonged indirectly to the château, where he was born at the time when his father was the Saint-Fiacres' steward. I warned you, Maître ... It was you who insisted ...'

It was ten o'clock. Maigret calculated that Marie Vassilief's train must have arrived half an hour earlier at the Gare de Lyon.

'Excuse me,' he said. 'I'll see you later.'

'But ...'

He in his turn went into the grocer's over the way, making the bell ring as he entered. He had to wait for a quarter of an hour to get through to Paris.

'Is it true that you're the old steward's son?'

Maigret was more tired than after ten normal cases. He felt utterly exhausted, both morally and physically.

'You're through to Paris ...'

'Hullo ... The Comptoir d'Escompte? ... This is Police Headquarters ... Some information ... Was a cheque signed Saint-Fiacre presented this morning? ... What's that? ... It was presented at nine o'clock and there were no funds to meet it? ... Hullo? ... Don't cut us off, Mademoiselle ... You asked the bearer to present it again? ... Excellent! ... Ah, that's what I wanted to know ... A young woman, wasn't it? ... A quarter of an hour ago? ... And she paid in the forty thousand francs? ... Thank you ... Yes, of course. Pay up ... No, no, there's nothing wrong ... Seeing that the money has been paid in ...'

And Maigret came out of the call-box heaving a weary sigh.

During the night, Maurice de Saint-Fiacre had found the forty thousand francs and he had sent his mistress to Paris to pay them into the bank.

Just as the chief-inspector was leaving the grocer's he caught sight of the priest coming out of the presbytery, with his breviary in his hand, and making for the château.

He quickened his pace, and almost ran to reach the door at the same time as the priest.

He missed him by less than a minute. When he reached the courtyard, the door was closing on the Curé. And when he rang the bell, he heard footsteps at the far end of the corridor, going in the direction of the library.

6 The Two Camps

'I'll see if Monsieur le Comte can . . .'

But the chief-inspector did not give the butler time to finish his sentence. He went into the corridor and made for the library while the butler gave a sigh of resignation. It was no longer even possible to keep up appearances! People came and went as if they were in a shop. Things had come to a pretty pass . . .

Maigret paused before opening the library door, but it was in vain, for he could not hear anything. Indeed, that was what made his entrance rather impressive.

He knocked, thinking that the priest might be somewhere else. But a voice, very firm and very clear in the silence of the room, replied immediately:

'Come in!'

Maigret pushed open the door, stopping accidentally on a heating vent. Standing in front of him, leaning lightly against the Gothic table, the Comte de Saint-Fiacre was looking at him.

Beside him, staring at the carpet, the priest remained absolutely still, as if the slightest movement would have driven him away.

What were the two of them doing there, neither speaking nor moving? It would have been less embarrassing to interrupt a pathetic scene than to break into a silence so profound that the human voice seemed to trace concentric circles in it, like a pebble in a pool of water.

Once again, Maigret felt conscious of Saint-Fiacre's

weariness. As for the priest, he looked stunned, and his fingers were twitching on his breviary.

'Excuse me for disturbing you . . .'

His words sounded sarcastic and yet he did not mean them to be. But was it possible to disturb people who were as inert as inanimate objects?

'I have some news from the bank . . .'

The count's gaze rested on the priest and that gaze was hard, almost furious.

The whole scene was to continue in the same vein. It was as if the characters were chess players thinking with their foreheads in their hands, remaining silent for several minutes before moving a pawn, and then returning to immobility.

But it was not thought which was immobilizing them like that. Maigret was convinced that it was fear of making a false move, a clumsy manoeuvre. Between the two of them there was a misunderstanding. And each one was reluctant to move his pawn, ready to take it back.

'I came to get instructions for the funeral,' the priest felt it necessary to say.

That was not true. A pawn had been badly placed. So badly placed that the Comte de Saint-Fiacre smiled.

'I guessed that you would telephone to the bank,' he said. 'And I am going to tell you why I decided to take that step. It was to get rid of Marie Vassilief, who did not want to leave the château . . . I persuaded her that it was absolutely essential . . .'

In the priest's eyes, now, Maigret could read anguish and disapproval.

'The poor wretch!' he must have been thinking. 'He has let himself be caught. He has fallen into the trap. He is done for . . .'

Silence. The scraping of a match and the puffs of smoke which the chief-inspector blew out one after another as he asked:

71

'Gautier found the money?'

A very short pause.

'No, Chief-Inspector . . . I'm going to tell you . . .'

It was not on Saint-Fiacre's face that the drama was being enacted: it was on the priest's. He was pale. His lips had a bitter twist to them. He was making an effort not to intervene.

'Listen, Monsieur . . .'

He could not stand it any longer.

'Would you mind interrupting this conversation until we've had a talk together?'

The same smile as before on Maurice's lips. It was cold in the huge room where the finest books in the library were missing. A fire had been laid in the hearth. It just needed a match.

'Have you a lighter or . . .'

And while he was bending over the hearth, the priest darted a miserable, beseeching look at Maigret.

'No,' said the count, returning towards the two men, 'I'm going to clear up the situation in a few words. For some reason which I don't know, Monsieur le Curé, who is full of good will, is convinced that it was I who . . . why should I be afraid of words? . . . who killed my mother! . . . For it was definitely a crime, wasn't it, even if it doesn't quite fall within the jurisdiction of the law . . .'

The priest was no longer moving, maintaining that trembling immobility of the animal which feels some danger approaching and cannot face it.

'Monsieur le Curé must have been very devoted to my mother . . . He probably wished to avoid the château being involved in a scandal . . . Last night he sent the sacristan to me with forty thousand francs in cash as well as a little note . . .'

Without any possible doubt, the expression in the priest's eyes was saying:

72

'Fool! You are done for!'

'Here is the note,' Saint-Fiacre went on.

Maigret read in an undertone:

'Be careful. I am praying for you.'

*

Whew! It was like the effect of a gust of fresh air. Straight away, Maurice de Saint-Fiacre ceased to feel rooted to the spot, condemned to immobility. He also lost that gravity which was contrary to his nature.

He started walking up and down, speaking in a lighter voice.

'That, Chief-Inspector, is why you saw me prowling round the church and the presbytery this morning ... I accepted the forty thousand francs, which must obviously be regarded as a loan, first of all, as I have told you, to get my mistress out of the way – excuse me, Monsieur le Curé – and then because it would have been extremely unpleasant to have been arrested at this moment ... But we are all remaining standing as if ... Do sit down, please ...'

He went over to the door, opened it and listened to a noise on the floor above.

'The procession is starting again!' he murmured. 'I think we'll have to telephone to Moulins to have a mortuary chapel installed ...' Then he went straight on:

'I suppose you understand it now? Once I had accepted the money, it remained for me to swear to Monsieur le Curé that I was not guilty. It was difficult for me to do that in front of you, Chief-Inspector, without making you even more suspicious ... That's all! .. This morning, as if you could read my thoughts, you didn't leave me alone for a moment, in the vicinity of the church ... Then Monsieur le Curé came here, I don't yet know why, for when you came in he was hesitating to speak ...'

73

His eyes clouded over. To shake off the bitterness which was assailing him, he laughed, a painful laugh.

'It's simple, isn't it? A man who has led a gay life and signed bad cheques ... Old Gautier is avoiding me! ... He too must be convinced that ...'

Suddenly he looked at the priest in astonishment.

'Well, Monsieur le Curé ... What's the matter?'

The priest, sure enough, looked gloomy. His gaze avoided the young man, and also tried to avoid Maigret's eyes.

Maurice de Saint-Fiacre understood, and exclaimed even more bitterly:

'There you are! You still don't believe me ... And it's the very man who wants to help me who is convinced of my guilt ...'

He went and opened the door once again, and, forgetting the presence of the dead woman in the house, called out:

'Albert! ... Albert! ... Look sharp, man! ... Bring us something to drink ...'

The butler came in, and went over to a cupboard from which he took a decanter of whisky and some glasses. Nobody said anything. They watched him. Maurice de Saint-Fiacre observed with a peculiar smile:

'In my time, there was no whisky in the château.'

'It was Monsieur Jean ...'

'Ah!'

He took a long drink, and then went and locked the door behind the butler.

'There are lots of things like that which have changed,' he muttered to himself.

But he did not take his eyes off the priest, and the latter, feeling increasingly ill at ease, stammered:

'Please excuse me ... I must go to my catechism class ...'

'Just a moment ... You are still convinced of my

74

guilt, Monsieur le Curé ... No, don't deny it ... Priests are no good at lying ... Only there are a few points I would like to clear up ... Because you don't know me ... You weren't at Saint-Fiacre in my time ... You've only heard people talking about me ... There are no material clues ... The chief-inspector, who was there when it happened, knows something about it ...'

'I beg you ...' stammered the priest.

'No! ... You won't have anything to drink? ... Good health, Chief-Inspector ...'

His gaze was sombre. He pursued his train of thought with fierce intensity.

'There are lots of people you could suspect ... But it's I whom you suspect, and I alone ... And I keep wondering why ... That's what prevented me from sleeping last night ... I thought of all the possible reasons and now I think I know ... What did my mother tell you?'

This time the priest went white.

'I don't know anything,' he stammered.

'Come now, Monsieur le Curé ... You have helped me, I agree ... You have let me have those forty thousand francs which will grant me a breathing-space and allow me to give my mother a decent burial ... I thank you with all my heart ... Only, at the same time, you regard me with suspicion ... You pray for me ... That's either too much or not enough ...'

The voice began to take on a tone of anger and menace.

'First of all I thought of having this talk with you outside Monsieur Maigret's presence ... Well, now I'm glad that he is here ... The more I think about it, the more I detect something odd going on ...'

'Monsieur le Comte, I implore you not to torture me any more ...'

'And I for my part, Monsieur le Curé, warn you that you won't leave this room until you have told me the truth!'

75

He was a changed man. He was at the end of his tether. And, like all weak and gentle people, he had turned unduly fierce.

His voice must have been audible in the dead woman's room, which was just above the library.

'You were on good terms with my mother ... I suppose that Jean Métayer was one of your parishioners too ... Which of the two said something? ... My mother, wasn't it?'

Maigret remembered the words he had heard the day before:

'The seal of the confessional ...'

He understood the priest's torment, his anguish, his martyred expression under the avalanche of Saint-Fiacre's words.

'What did she say to you? ... I knew her, you know! ... I was present, so to speak, at the beginning of the decline ... All of us here know what life is like ...'

He looked around him with unspoken anger.

'There was a time,' he said, 'when people held their breath when they came into this room, because my father, *the master*, was working here. There was no whisky in the cupboards ... But the shelves were loaded with books as the cells of a beehive are saturated with honey ...'

Maigret remembered that too.

'*The count is working* ...'

And those words were enough to keep farmers waiting for two hours in the anteroom.

'*The count called me into the library* ...'

And Maigret's father was impressed by this summons because for him it was an important event.

'He didn't waste logs, but managed with a paraffin stove which he put close to him, to help out the central heating,' said Maurice de Saint-Fiacre.

And, speaking to the distraught priest, he went on:

76

'You never saw that ... You only saw the château in its decline ... My mother who had lost her husband .. My mother whose only son was making a fool of himself in Paris and never came here except to ask for money ... And then there were the secretaries ...'

His pupils were so bright that Maigret expected to see tears begin to flow.

'What did she say to you? ... She was afraid of seeing me arrive, wasn't she? ... She knew that there would be some new debts to pay off, that something else would have to be sold to save me once again ...'

'You ought to calm down,' the priest said in a dull voice.

'Not before knowing ... whether you suspected me without knowing me, right from the start ...'

Maigret intervened.

'Monsieur le Curé had hidden the missal,' he said slowly.

He for his part had already understood. He was holding out a helping hand to Saint-Fiacre. He could imagine the countess, torn between sin and remorse ... Wasn't she afraid of being punished? ... Wasn't she a little ashamed in front of her son?

She was a sick woman, easily worried. And it was quite possible that under the seal of the confessional she had said one day:

'I'm afraid of my son ...'

For she must have been afraid. The money which went to Jean Métayer and his like was Saint-Fiacre money which rightly belonged to Maurice. Wouldn't he call her to account for it one day? Wouldn't ...

Maigret was conscious that these ideas were beginning to occur to the young man, though as yet in a confused form. He was helping to clarify them.

'Monsieur le Curé cannot say anything if the countess spoke under the seal of the confessional ...'

That was clear. Maurice de Saint-Fiacre cut the conversation short.

'Forgive me, Monsieur le Curé ... I was forgetting your catechism class ... Please don't hold it against me if ...'

He turned the key in the lock and opened the door.

'Thank you ... As soon as ... as soon as possible, I will return the forty thousand francs to you ... For I imagine that they don't belong to you ...'

'I asked Madame Ruinard, the widow of the former solicitor, for them ...'

'Thank you ... Good-bye ...'

He nearly slammed the door shut, but he restrained himself, looked Maigret in the eyes and snarled:

'What a filthy business!'

'He wanted to ...'

'He wanted to save me, I know! ... He tried to avoid a scandal, to stick the pieces of the château de Saint-Fiacre back together again as best he could ... It isn't that ...'

And he poured out some whisky.

'I'm thinking of that poor woman ... Look, you have seen Marie Vassilief ... And all the other women of Paris ... They don't have attacks of conscience ... But my mother! ... And remember that what she was looking for above all else, with that fellow Métayer, was a chance to give her affection ... Then she would rush off to the confessional ... She must have regarded herself as a monster ... From that to fearing my vengeance ... Ha! Ha! ...'

That laughter of his was terrifying to hear.

'Can you see me, an indignant son, attacking my mother for ... And that priest didn't understand! ... He sees life in terms of the Scriptures ... While my mother was alive, he must have tried to save her from herself ... Once she was dead, he thought it his duty to save me ...

But at this moment I'm willing to bet that he's convinced it was I who ...'

He looked the chief-inspector in the eyes and asked:

'And what about you?'

And as Maigret made no reply he went on:

'For there has been a crime ... A crime which only the filthiest swine imaginable could have committed ... The dirty little coward! ... Is it true that the Law can do nothing against him? ... I heard something to that effect this morning ... But I'm going to tell you something, Chief-Inspector, and you can take it down and use it against me ... When I find that little swine, well, well, he'll have to deal with me, and me alone ... And I won't need a revolver! No, no weapon at all ... Nothing but these two hands ...'

The whisky was obviously making him more excited. He noticed that, for he passed his hand over his forehead, looked at himself in the mirror, and pulled a mocking face at himself.

'The fact remains, if it hadn't been for the priest, I'd be in prison even before the funeral! I wasn't very nice to him ... And the wife of the former solicitor, who has paid my debts ... Who is she? ... I can't remember ...'

'The lady who always dresses in white ... The house which has a gate with gilded spikes, on the road to Matignon ...'

Maurice de Saint-Fiacre began to calm down. His outburst had been only a flash in the pan. He began to pour out a drink for himself, hesitated, and swallowed the contents of his glass at one draught, with a grimace of disgust.

'Can you hear that?'

'What?'

'The local people filing past upstairs ... I ought to be there, in deep mourning, red-eyed, shaking their hands with a heart-broken air ... Once outside, they start talking ...'

79

He added suspiciously:

'Now I come to think of it, if, as you say, the Law is not concerned with the case, why are you staying here?'

'Something new might turn up ...'

'And if I found the culprit, would you prevent me from ...'

The clenched fingers were more eloquent than any speech.

'I must leave you,' said Maigret. 'I have to go and have a look at the other camp ...'

'The other camp?'

'The one at the inn. Jean Métayer and his lawyer, who arrived this morning ...

'He's called in a lawyer?'

'He's a thoughtful fellow ... This morning the two sides were lined up like this: at the château, you and the priest; at the inn, the young man and his adviser ...'

'You think he could have been capable ...?'

'May I help myself?'

And Maigret drank a glass of whisky, wiped his lips, and filled a last pipe before leaving.

'I suppose you don't know how to use a linotype?'

A shrug of the shoulders.

'I don't know how to use anything ... That's the trouble ...'

'You won't, under any circumstances, leave the village without informing me, will you?'

A grave, deep look. And a grave, deep voice:

'I give you my word.'

*

Maigret went out. He was about to go down the outside steps when a man appeared beside him before he could see where he had come from.

'Excuse me, Chief-Inspector ... Could you spare me a few minutes? ... I've been told ...'

'What?'

'That you practically belong to the house ... Your father was in my job ... Would you do me the honour of having a drink with me at home?'

And the grey-bearded steward led his companion across the yards. Everything was ready in his house. A bottle of brandy whose label proclaimed its great age. Biscuits. A smell of cabbages and bacon was coming from the kitchen.

'From what I've heard, you knew the château in very different circumstances ... When I arrived here the decline was beginning ... There was a young man from Paris who ... This is some brandy from the days of the late count ... No sugar, I suppose?'

Maigret stared at the table with the carved lions which had brass rings in their mouths. And once again he felt physically and morally tired. In the old days, he had only been allowed to come into this room if he was wearing slippers, on account of the polished floor.

'I'm in a rather difficult position ... And it's you I'd like to ask for advice ... We are poor people ... You know that a steward's job doesn't make a man rich ...

'Some Saturdays when there wasn't any money in the safe, I paid the farmers myself ...

'At other times, I advanced money to buy cattle the tenant farmers wanted ...'

'In other words, the countess owed you money!'

'Madame la Comtesse knew nothing about business ... Money was disappearing all over the place ... It was only for indispensable things that it wasn't available ...'

'And it was you ...'

'Your father would have done the same, wouldn't he? There are times when you mustn't let the local people see that the coffers are empty ... I drew on my savings ...'

MGH—6

'How much?'

'Another glass? ... I haven't counted ... At least seventy thousand ... And now again for the funeral, it's I who ...'

A picture imposed itself on Maigret's mind:

His father's little office near the stables, at five o'clock on Saturday. All the people employed at the château, from the linen maids to the farm labourers, were waiting outside. And old Maigret, installed behind the desk covered with green percale, was arranging coins in little heaps. Each peasant passed by in turn, and signed his name or made a cross on the register ...

'Now I don't know how I'm going to get it back ... For people like us, it's ...'

'Yes, I understand ... You've had the mantelpiece changed?'

'Yes, the old one was in wood ... Marble looks better ...'

'Much better!' grunted Maigret.

'You understand, don't you? All the creditors are going to descend on the château ... The count will have to sell up ... And with the mortgages ...'

The armchair in which Maigret was sitting was new, like the mantelpiece, and must have come from a Paris furniture shop. There was a gramophone on the sideboard.

'If I hadn't a son, I wouldn't mind, but Emile has his career to think about ... I don't want to rush matters ...'

A girl walked along the corridor.

'You have a daughter too?'

'No. That's a local girl who comes in to do the heavy work.'

'Well, we'll talk about this another time, Monsieur Gautier. Excuse me. I've still a lot of things to do ...'

'Another glass?'

'No, thank you ... You said about seventy-five thousand, didn't you?'

And he went off, his hands in his pockets, threaded his way through the flocks of geese, and walked along by the Notre-Dame pond where the water had stopped lapping ... The church clock struck noon.

At Marie Tatin's, Jean Métayer and the lawyer were eating. They were having sardines, fillets of herring, and sausage, as *hors d'œuvre*. On the next table, there were the glasses which had contained their apéritifs.

The two men were in high spirits. They greeted Maigret with sarcastic glances. They winked at each other. The lawyer's briefcase was closed once more.

'I hope at least you've found some truffles for the chicken?' said Maître Tallier.

Poor Marie Tatin! She had found a tiny tin of truffles at the grocer's, but she could not manage to open it and she did not dare to admit this.

'Yes, I've found some, Monsieur.'

'Then hurry up! The air here makes a man terribly hungry ...'

It was Maigret who went to the kitchen and, with his penknife, cut open the tin while the woman with the squint stammered in an undertone:

'I don't know what to say ... I ...'

'Shut up, Marie!' he growled.

One camp ... Two camps ... Three camps?

He felt a need to make a joke in order to forget the realities of the situation.

'By the way, the priest asked me to bring you three hundred days' indulgence. To count against your sins!'

And Marie Tatin, who did not understand the joke, gazed at her burly companion with a mixture of fear and affectionate respect.

Maigret had telephoned to Moulins to order a taxi. He was surprised at first to see one arrive barely ten minutes after his telephone call, but as he was making for the door, the lawyer, who was just finishing his coffee, intervened.

'Excuse me! That's ours ... But if you want a lift ...'

'No, thank you ...'

Jean Métayer and the lawyer left first in a big car which still bore the coat of arms of its former owner. A quarter of an hour later, Maigret went off in his turn, and on the way, while he was chatting with the driver, he looked at the countryside.

The scenery was monotonous: two rows of poplars along the road, and ploughed fields stretching away as far as the eye could see, with here and there a rectangular thicket or the blue-green eye of a pond.

The houses were for the most part just cottages. And that was understandable, since there were no small landowners.

Nothing but big estates, one of which, that of the Duc de T—, contained three villages.

The Saint-Fiacre estate had covered five thousand acres, before the successive sales.

The only means of transport was an old Paris bus which had been bought by a peasant and which covered the distance between Moulins and Saint-Fiacre once a day.

'This is real country for you!' said the taxi-driver. 'It's all right now. But in the depths of winter ...'

They drove down the high street of Moulins with the hands of the clock of Saint-Pierre standing at half past two. Maigret asked the driver to stop in front of the Comptoir d'Escompte and paid the fare. Just as he was turning away from the taxi to make for the bank, a woman came out of the building holding a little boy by the hand.

The chief-inspector hurriedly looked into a shop-window so as not to be noticed. The woman was a peasant woman in her Sunday best, her hat balancing on her hair, her waist constricted by a corset. She was walking along in a dignified manner, trailing the little boy behind her, without taking any more notice of him than she would of a parcel.

It was Ernest, the red-haired boy who served Mass at Saint-Fiacre.

The street was crowded. Ernest would have liked to stop at each window, but he was towed along in the wake of the black skirt. However, his mother bent down to say something to him. And, as if it had been decided in advance, she went into a toy shop with him.

Maigret did not dare to get too close. All the same, he gathered what was happening from the whistle blasts which soon started coming from the shop. Every imaginable whistle was tried in turn, and finally the choirboy must have decided on a boy-scout whistle with two notes.

When he came out, he was wearing it on a string around his neck, but his mother pulled him along, preventing him from blowing it in the street.

*

A bank like any other in a small country town. A long oak counter. Five clerks bent over desks. Maigret made for the section of the counter marked *Current Accounts*, and one of the clerks stood up to serve him.

Maigret wanted to inquire about the exact state of the Saint-Fiacres' fortune, and above all about any deposits or withdrawals in the last few weeks, or even the last few days, which might provide him with a clue.

But for a moment he said nothing, simply looking at the young man, who maintained a respectful attitude, without showing any sign of impatience.

'Emile Gautier, I suppose?'

He had seen him go past twice on a motorcycle but he had been unable to distinguish his features. What had revealed the bank clerk's identity to him was a striking resemblance to the steward of the château.

Not so much a resemblance of details as a resemblance of race. The same peasant origins: clear-cut features and big bones.

The same degree of evolution, more or less, revealed by a skin which was rather better cared-for than that of the farm workers, by intelligent eyes, and by a self-assurance which was that of an 'educated man'.

But Emile was not yet a townsman. His hair, although covered with brilliantine, remained rebellious, and stood up in a spike on the top of his head. His cheeks were pink, with that well-scrubbed look of country yokels on Sunday morning.

'That is correct.'

He was not at all flustered. Maigret was already sure that he was a model employee, in whom his manager had complete trust, and who would soon obtain promotion.

A black suit, made to measure, but by a local tailor, in a serge which would never wear out. His father wore a celluloid collar. He for his part wore a soft collar, but his tie was ready-tied.

'Do you know me?'

'No. I suppose that you are the police officer ...'

'And I would like some information about the state of the Saint-Fiacre account.'

'That's a simple matter. I am in charge of that account as well as all the others.'

He was polite, well-mannered. At school, he must have been the teachers' favourite.

'Pass me the Saint-Fiacre account,' he said to a girl clerk sitting behind him.

And he let his gaze wander over a big sheet of yellow paper.

'Is it a summary that you want, the amount of the balance, or some general information?'

At least he was precise!

'Is the account in a healthy state?'

'Come this way, will you? ... Somebody might hear us here ...'

They went off to the far end of the room, although still separated by the oak counter.

'My father must have told you that the countess was very unmethodical ... Time and again, I had to stop cheques which could not be met . . Mind you, she didn't know that ... She used to make out cheques without worrying about the state of her account ... So that when I telephoned her to tell her, she would get into a panic ... This morning again, three cheques were presented and I am obliged to return them ... I have instructions to pay nothing out until ...'

'The family is completely ruined?'

'Not really ... Three farms out of five have been sold ... The other two are mortgaged, like the château ... The countess owned a block of flats in Paris, and that used to bring in a small income ... But then, all of a sudden, she would throw everything off balance ... I've always done the best I could ... I've had bills delayed two or three times ... My father ...'

'Has advanced money, I know.'

'That's all I can tell you ... At the moment, the credit balance stands at exactly seven hundred and seventy five francs ... Mind you, last year's land tax hasn't been paid, and the inspector issued a first warning last week ...'

'Is Jean Métayer aware of all this?'

'Yes. Indeed, more than just aware of it.'

'What do you mean?'

'Nothing.'

'You don't think he's living in the clouds?'

But Emile Gautier discreetly avoided making any reply.

'Is that all you want to know?'

'Are there any other inhabitants of Saint-Fiacre who have an account at this branch?'

'No.'

'And nobody has been here today to transact any business? To cash a cheque, for example?'

'Nobody.'

'And you have been here all the time?'

'I haven't moved from this counter.'

He was in no way discomposed. He remained a good employee answering the questions of a government official with due courtesy.

'Would you like to see the manager? Not that he could tell you any more than I can ...'

*

The lamps were lighting up. The high street was almost as crowded as in a big city, and there were long lines of cars in front of the cafés.

A procession went by: two camels and a young elephant carrying advertisements for a circus installed in the Place de la Victoire.

In the grocer's shop, Maigret caught sight of the red-haired boy's mother, who was still holding her son by the hand and who was buying tins of food.

A little farther on, he nearly bumped into Métayer and

his lawyer, who were walking along with a self-important air, talking together. The lawyer was saying:

'. . . they are obliged to freeze it . . .'

They did not see the chief-inspector and they continued on their way towards the Comptoir d'Escompte.

People are bound to run into each other a dozen times in an afternoon in a town where all the activity is concentrated in a street five hundred yards long.

Maigret made his way to the *Journal de Moulins* building. The offices were at the front: a concrete façade and modern plateglass windows with a lavish display of press photographs and the latest news written out in blue pencil on long strips of paper.

'Manchuria. The Havas Agency reports that . . .'

But to reach the printing house, Maigret had to go down a dark cul-de-sac, guided by the din of the rotary press. In a dismal workshop some men in overalls were working at the tall stone-topped tables. In a glass cage at the far end there were the two linotypes with their machine-gun rattle.

'The foreman, please . . .'

He literally had to yell, on account of the thunder of the machines. The smell of ink took him by the throat. A short man in blue overalls who was arranging lines of type in a forme cupped his hand round his ear.

'Are you the foreman?'

'The stone hand.'

Maigret took out of his wallet the piece of paper which had killed the Comtesse de Saint-Fiacre. The man settled his steel-rimmed spectacles on his nose and looked at it, obviously wondering what it was all about.

'Was this printed here?'

'What?'

Some people went past carrying piles of newspapers.

'I asked you whether this was printed here.'

'Come with me!'

It was better in the yard. It was cold there, but at least they could talk in more or less normal voices.

'What were you asking me?'

'Do you recognize this type?'

'It's Cheltenham nine point . . .'

'From here?'

'Nearly all linotypes are fitted with Cheltenham.'

'Are there any other linotypes at Moulins?'

'Not at Moulins . . . But at Nevers, Bourges, Châteauroux, Autun, and . . .'

'Do you notice anything special about this piece of paper?'

'It's only a proof . . . Whoever did it wanted to make it look like a newspaper cutting, didn't they? . . . Somebody once asked me to do the same thing, for a joke . . .'

'Ah!'

'At least fifteen years ago . . . In the days when we still set the newspaper by hand . . .'

'And the paper doesn't tell you anything?'

'Nearly all provincial newspapers have the same supplier. It's German paper . . . Will you excuse me? . . . I've got to lock the forme . . . It's for the Nièvre edition . . .'

'Do you know Jean Métayer?'

The man shrugged his shoulders.

'What do you think of him?'

'If you take his word for it, he knows the business better than we do. He's a bit cracked . . . We let him mess about in the workshop because of the countess, who's a friend of the boss . . .'

'Does he know how to work a linotype?'

'Hmm! . . . He says so . . .'

'Well, would he be capable of setting this news item?'

'With a good two hours in front of him . . . And starting the same line over and over again . . .'

'Has he sat down at a linotype recently?'

'How do I know? He comes and goes all the time, bothering us with his photos ... Excuse me ... The train won't wait ... And I haven't locked my forme ...'

There was no point in persisting. Maigret nearly went back into the workshop, but the frantic activity inside discouraged him. Every minute counted for these people. Everybody was running around. The porters elbowed him aside as they dashed towards the gate.

All the same, he managed to button-hole an apprentice who was rolling a cigarette.

'What do you do with the lines of metal when they've been used?'

'We melt them down.'

'How often?'

'Every other day ... Look, the metal pot is over there in the corner ... Mind out! ... It's hot ...'

Maigret went out a little weary, perhaps a little discouraged. Darkness had fallen. The roadway was bright, brighter than usual, because of the cold. In front of a tailor's shop, a salesman who was stamping his feet and had a cold in the head was accosting the passers-by.

'A winter overcoat? ... Fine English cloth from two hundred francs ... Come inside! There's no obligation to buy ...'

A little farther on, outside the Café de Paris, where billiard balls could be heard colliding, Maigret saw the Comte de Saint-Fiacre's yellow car.

He went in, looked around for the man, and, failing to see him, sat down on a bench. It was the smart café of the town. On the platform, three musicians were tuning their instruments and setting out the number of the next piece with the help of three pieces of cardboard, each of which bore a figure.

There was some noise coming from the call-box.

'A beer,' Maigret told the waiter.

'Light or dark?'

But the chief-inspector was trying to hear the voice in the call-box. He failed to do so. Saint-Fiacre came out and the cashier asked him:

'How many calls?'

'Three.'

'To Paris, weren't they? ... Three times eight is twenty-four ...'

The count caught sight of Maigret, walked over to him quite naturally, and sat down beside him.

'You didn't tell me you were coming to Moulins ... I'd have driven you over in my car ... It's true it's an open car and in this weather ...'

'Did you telephone Marie Vassilief?'

'No. I don't see why I should hide the truth from you .. A beer for me too, waiter ... Or rather no! Something hot ... A grog ... I telephoned a certain Monsieur Wolf ... If you don't know him, others are bound to, at the Quai des Orfèvres ... He's a money-lender ... I've had recourse to him a few times ... I've just been trying to ...'

Maigret looked at him inquisitively.

'You asked him for some money?'

'At any rate of interest he liked! He refused, incidentally ... Don't look at me like that! I dropped into the bank this afternoon ...'

'At what time?'

'About three o'clock ... That young man and his lawyer were just coming out ...'

'You tried to withdraw some money?'

'I tried, yes! Now don't imagine that I want to arouse your pity! There are some people who get embarrassed by anything to do with money. I don't ... Well, after sending the forty thousand to Paris and buying Marie Vassilief's ticket, I'm left with about three hundred francs in hand. I arrived here without expecting anything like this to happen ... I've nothing but the clothes I'm wearing now ... In Paris I owe a few thousand francs to the owner of my flat, and she won't send down any of my things ...'

As he spoke he watched the balls rolling across the green cloth of the billiard-table. The players were humble youths of the town who cast envious glances now and then at the count's elegant suit.

'That's all! I would at least have liked to be in mourning for the funeral. There isn't a tailor round here who would give me credit for a couple of days. At the bank I was told that my mother's account was frozen and that in any case the credit balance amounted to just over seven hundred francs ... And do you know who gave me that agreeable information?'

'Your steward's son.'

'Right!'

He drank a mouthful of scalding grog and fell silent, still looking at the billiard-table. The orchestra struck up a Viennese waltz which was given a curious accompaniment by the sound of the balls.

It was hot. The light in the café was rather dim, in spite of the electric lamps. It was a typical provincial café, with only one concession to modern times, a notice advertising : *Cocktails 6 francs.*

Maigret puffed slowly at his pipe. He too gazed at the billiard-table, which was crudely lit by lamps with green cardboard shades. Now and then the door opened and after a few seconds a gust of icy air would reach him.

'Let's go and sit at the back ...'

It was the voice of the lawyer from Bourges. He passed in front of the table where the two men were sitting, followed by Jean Métayer who was wearing white woollen gloves. But both of them were looking straight ahead. They did not see the first pair until they had sat down.

The two tables were practically facing each other.

There was a slight flush in Métayer's cheeks, and his voice trembled as he gave his order:

'A chocolate.'

Saint-Fiacre commented jokingly in an undertone:

'That's right, darling!'

A woman sat down at an equal distance from the two tables, gave a friendly smile to the waiter, and murmured:

'The usual!'

He brought her a cherry brandy. She powdered her face and touched up her lipstick, fluttering her eyelids and wondering whether to direct her gaze towards one table or the other.

Was it burly, easy-going Maigret whom she ought to attack? Or was it the more elegant lawyer, who was already looking her up and down with a little smile?

'Well, there it is! I'll have to lead the mourners in grey!' murmured the Comte de Saint-Fiacre. 'After all, I can't very well borrow a black suit from the butler or put on one of my late father's tailcoats!'

Apart from the lawyer, who was interested by the woman, everybody was looking at the nearest billiard table.

There were three tables in all. Two were occupied. There were a few cheers just as the musicians were finishing their number. And straight away, the sounds of glasses and saucers could be heard again.

'Three ports!'

The door kept opening and shutting. The cold air came in, and was gradually absorbed by the prevailing warmth.

The lamps over the third billiard-table lit up at a gesture from the cashier, who had the electric switches behind her.

'Thirty points!'

And speaking to the waiter, the same voice added:

'A quarter of Vichy ... No! A strawberry Vittel ...'

It was Emile Gautier, who was carefully coating the tip of his cue with blue chalk. Then he put the marker at zero. His companion was the assistant manager of the bank, a man ten years older, with a waxed moustache.

It was only at the third stroke – which he muffed – that the young man caught sight of Maigret. He greeted him, looking a little embarrassed. After that, he was so absorbed in the game that he no longer had the time to see anybody at all.

'Of course, if you're not afraid of the cold, I can give you a lift in my car,' said Maurice de Saint-Fiacre. 'May I offer you a drink? One apéritif more or less won't ruin me, you know ...'

'Waiter!' Jean Métayer called out. 'Get me Bourges seventeen on the telephone!'

His father's number! A little later, he shut himself up in the call-box.

Maigret went on smoking. He had ordered another beer. And the woman, possibly because he was the fattest of the four men, had finally chosen him. Every time he turned in her direction, she smiled at him as if they were old acquaintances.

She could not have known that he was thinking about 'the old girl', as the son himself called her, who was laid out on the first floor of the château back at Saint-Fiacre, with the peasants filing in front of her and nudging one another in the ribs.

But it was not in those circumstances that he was picturing her. He was seeing her at a time when there were no cars yet in front of the Café de Paris and nobody drank cocktails there.

In the park of the château, a tall lithe thorough-bred, like the heroine of a popular novel, beside the baby-carriage being pushed along by the nursemaid ...

Maigret was just a youngster whose hair, like that of

Emile Gautier and the red-haired choirboy, insisted on standing up in a spike on the top of his head.

Wasn't he jealous of the count that morning when the couple left for Aix-les-Bains in a motor-car (one of the first he had seen) full of furs and scent? The face behind the veil was invisible. The count was wearing huge goggles. It was all like an heroic elopement. And the nanny held the baby's hand and waved it in farewell ...

Now they were sprinkling the old woman with holy water and the bedroom smelt of candles.

Emile Gautier circled round the billiard-table, played a fancy shot and counted solemnly in an undertone:

'Seven ...'

He bent down again, He pulled off another shot. The assistant manager with the waxed moustache said in a sour voice:

'Magnificent!'

Two men eyed each other across the green cloth: Jean Métayer, to whom the smiling lawyer was talking incessantly, and the Comte de Saint-Fiacre, who stopped the waiter with an elegant gesture.

'The same again!'

Maigret, for his part, was thinking now of a boy-scout whistle. A splendid bronze whistle with two notes, such as he had never possessed himself.

8   The Invitation to Dinner

'Another telephone call!' sighed Maigret as he saw Métayer stand up once more.

He followed him with his eyes, noting that he did not go into either the call-box or the toilets. Moreover, the plump lawyer was now sitting on the very edge of his chair like somebody who is wondering whether to get up. He was looking at the Comte de Saint-Fiacre. You might almost have thought that he was about to venture a smile.

Was it Maigret who was in the way? In any case, this scene reminded the chief-inspector of certain incidents in his youth: three or four friends in a café together, and two women at the other end of the room. The discussions, the hesitations, the waiter you called to entrust him with a note ...

The lawyer was in the same state of nerves. And the woman sitting two tables away from Maigret misinterpreted it and thought that it was she who was responsible. She smiled, opened her handbag, and powdered her face.

'I'll be back in a moment,' the chief-inspector said to his companion.

He crossed the room in the direction Métayer had taken, and saw a door he had not noticed before which led into a wide corridor with a red carpet. At the far end there was a counter with a big book on it, a telephone switchboard and a girl receptionist. Métayer was there talking to the latter. He left her just as Maigret came forward.

'Thank you, Mademoiselle ... You say it's in the first street on the left?'

He made no attempt to hide from the chief-inspector. He did not seem to be embarrassed by his presence. On the contrary! And there was a gleam of joy in his eyes.

'I didn't know that this was a hotel,' Maigret said to the girl.

'You're staying somewhere else, then? ... That's a pity ... Because this is really the best hotel in Moulins ...'

'Haven't you had the Comte de Saint-Fiacre staying here?'

She nearly burst out laughing. Then she became serious all of a sudden.

'What's he done?' she asked with a certain anxiety. 'That's the second time in five minutes that ...'

'Where did you send the previous inquirer?'

'He wanted to know whether the Comte de Saint-Fiacre went out during Saturday night ... I couldn't tell him, because the night porter hasn't arrived yet ... Then the gentleman asked if we had a garage and he's gone over there ...'

So all that Maigret had to do was follow Métayer!

'And the garage is on the first street on the left,' he said, a little annoyed in spite of everything.

'That's right. It's open all night.'

Jean Métayer had certainly lost no time for when Maigret reached the street in question, he was coming out of the garage, whistling to himself. The attendant was eating a snack in one corner.

'It's for the same thing that gentleman has just asked you about ... The yellow car ... Did anybody come and take it out during Saturday night?'

There was already a ten-franc note on the table. Maigret put down another.

'Yes, about midnight.'

'And it was brought back?'

'About three o'clock in the morning ...'

'Was it dirty?'

'Not really ... The weather's been dry lately, you know.'

'There were two people, weren't there? A man and a woman ...'

'No! A man by himself.'

'Short and thin?'

'Not a bit of it! A big healthy fellow.'

Obviously the Comte de Saint-Fiacre ...

*

When Maigret went back into the café, the orchestra was playing again, and the first thing he noticed was that there was nobody left in the corner where Métayer and his companion had been sitting.

True, a few seconds later he spotted the lawyer sitting in his own seat, next to the Comte de Saint-Fiacre. At the sight of the chief-inspector he got up from the bench.

'Excuse me. No, do sit down here again, please ...'

He did not go away, however, but sat down on the chair opposite. He was very nervous, with flushed cheeks, like a man in a hurry to be done with a difficult task. His eyes seemed to be searching for Jean Métayer who was nowhere to be seen.

'I want you to understand, Chief-Inspector ... I wouldn't have taken the liberty of going to the château ... That goes without saying ... But since we have been brought together by chance on neutral territory, if I may say so ...'

And he gave a forced smile. After every sentence, he gave the impression of bowing to the other two men and thanking them for their approval.

'In a situation as painful as this, there is no point in complicating matters further, as I told my client, by being unduly sensitive ... Monsieur Jean Métayer understands this perfectly well ... And when you arrived, Chief-Inspector, I was saying to the Comte de Saint-Fiacre that we asked for nothing better than to come to an understanding ...'

Maigret growled:

'Well, I'll be damned!'

And he thought to himself:

'You, my good fellow, will be lucky if in the next five minutes you don't get the hand of the gentleman you're talking to so suavely right across your face ...'

The billiard-players went on circling round the tables. As for the woman, she stood up, leaving her handbag on the table, and went off towards the back of the room.

'There's another who's making a big mistake. She's just had a bright idea. Perhaps Métayer left the room so that he could speak to her outside without being seen? ... So off she goes to look for him ...'

Maigret was right. With one hand on her hip, the woman was walking up and down, looking for the young man.

The lawyer was still talking.

'There are some very complicated interests involved and we for our part are ready ...'

'To do what?' Saint-Fiacre broke in.

'But ... to ...'

He forgot it was not his glass which was in front of him, and he drank out of Maigret's to keep himself in countenance.

'I know that perhaps this isn't the best place ... Or the best moment ... But remember that we know better than anybody else the financial situation of ...'

'My mother! Go on ...'

'My client, with a tact which does him honour, decided to move into the inn ...'

The poor devil of a lawyer! His words, now that Maurice de Saint-Fiacre was gazing fixedly at him, were coming from his throat one by one, as if they needed to be dragged out.

'You do understand, don't you, Chief-Inspector? ... We know that there's a will in the solicitor's keeping ... Don't worry! Monsieur le Comte's rights are respected ... But Jean Métayer is a beneficiary all the same ... The financial situation is rather complicated ... My client is the only one who knows all about it ...'

Maigret admired Saint-Fiacre, who was managing to maintain an almost angelic composure. There was even a faint smile on his lips.

'Yes! He was a model secretary!' he said without any apparent irony.

'You must remember that he comes from a very good family and has had an excellent upbringing. I know his parents ... His father ...'

'Let's get back to the fortune, shall we?'

It was too good to be true. The lawyer could scarcely believe his ears.

'Will you allow me to offer you both drinks? ... Waiter! ... The same again, gentlemen? ... As for me, I'll have a lemon Raphaël ...'

Two tables away, the woman had returned glumly to her seat, for she had failed to find Métayer and had resigned herself to tackling the billiard-players.

'I was saying that my client is prepared to help you ... There are certain persons whom he distrusts ... He'll tell you himself that some rather shady operations have been carried out by people not over-burdened with scruples ... Anyway ...'

This was the hardest part ... In spite of everything, the lawyer had to swallow hard before going on ...

'You've found the château coffers empty ... But it's essential for your late lamented mother ...'

'Your late lamented mother!' Maigret repeated admiringly.

'Your late lamented mother,' the lawyer continued without batting an eyelid ... 'What was I saying? ... Oh, yes! That the funeral should be worthy of the Saint-Fiacres ... Pending the time when matters can be arranged in everybody's best interests, my client will see to it that ...'

'In other words, he will advance the money necessary for the funeral ... Is that what you mean?'

Maigret did not dare to look at the count. He fixed his gaze on Emile Gautier who was making another break and waited tensely for the explosion which was about to take place beside him.

But no! Saint-Fiacre had stood up. He was speaking to a new arrival.

'Do sit down at our table, Monsieur.'

It was Métayer who had just come in and to whom the lawyer had doubtless explained by signs that everything was going well.

'A lemon Raphaël too? ... Waiter!'

Applause broke out in the room, because the orchestral item was over. Once the noise had died down, the situation was more embarrassing than before, for voices sounded louder. There was now only the click of the ivory balls to break the silence.

'I told Monsieur le Comte, who understands perfectly ...'

'Who is the Raphaël for?'

'You came from Saint-Fiacre, didn't you, gentlemen? ... In that case, my car is at your disposal to take you back ... You'll find it rather a tight fit ... I'm already giving a lift to the chief-inspector ... How much, waiter? ... No, please! ... It's my round ...'

But the lawyer stood up and was pressing a hundred-franc note into the hand of the waiter, who asked:

'The lot?'

'Yes, yes!'

And the count said with his most gracious smile: 'It's really too charming of you.'

Emile Gautier, who watched the four of them go off, making way for each other at the door, was so surprised that he forgot to go on with his break.

The lawyer found himself in front, next to the count, who was driving. Behind, there was only just enough room for Jean Métayer beside Maigret.

It was cold. The headlamps were not bright enough. The car had no silencer, and this made conversation impossible.

Did Maurice de Saint-Fiacre usually drive at this speed? Or was he taking his little revenge? The fact remains that he covered the fifteen miles from Moulins to the château in less than a quarter of an hour, taking the bends on the brake, speeding through the darkness, and once only narrowly missing a cart which was in the middle of the road and which forced him to drive up on the bank.

Their faces were cut by the wind. Maigret had to grip the collar of his overcoat in both hands. They drove through the village without slowing down. It was as much as they could do to catch a glimpse of the light in the inn and then the church spire.

A sudden stop, which threw the occupants of the car against one another. They were at the foot of the steps. The servants could be seen eating in the basement kitchen. Somebody was roaring with laughter.

'Will you allow me, gentlemen, to invite you to dinner? ...'

Métayer and the lawyer looked at each other in hesitation. The count pushed them inside with a friendly tap on the shoulder.

'Come along now ... It's my turn, isn't it?'

And in the hall he added:

'Unfortunately it won't be very gay . . .'

Maigret would have liked to have a few words with him in private, but the other did not give him time and opened the door of the smoking-room.

'Will you excuse me for a few moments? . . . Have an apéritif while you're waiting . . . I've some orders to give . . . You know where the bottles are, don't you, Monsieur Métayer? . . . Is there anything drinkable left? . . .'

He pressed an electric bell-push. The butler was a long time coming, and arrived with his mouth full and his napkin in his hand.

Saint-Fiacre snatched it from him with a swift gesture.

'Send for the steward . . . Then get me the presbytery and the doctor's house on the telephone.'

And to the others he said:

'Will you excuse me?'

The telephone was in the hall, which, like the rest of the château, was poorly lit. Since there was no electricity at Saint-Fiacre, the château had to provide its own current and the generator was too weak. The bulbs, instead of giving off a white light, revealed reddish filaments, as in certain trams when they come to a halt.

The hall was full of great patches of dark shadow in which it was almost impossible to make out any objects.

'Hullo . . . Yes, I insist . . . Thank you, Doctor . . .'

The lawyer and Maigret were uneasy. But as yet they did not dare to admit their uneasiness to each other. It was Jean Métayer who broke the silence, to ask the chief-inspector:

'What can I offer you? . . . I don't think there's any port left . . . But there's some whisky . . .'

All the ground-floor rooms were in a row, separated by wide open doors. The dining-room first. Then the drawing-room. Then the smoking-room where the three men were waiting. And finally the library where the young man went to get the drinks.

'Hullo ... Yes ... Can I count on you? ... See you soon ...'

The count made some more calls, then walked along the corridor running alongside all the rooms, and went upstairs, where his footsteps stopped in the dead woman's bedroom.

Other, heavier footsteps, in the hall. A knock on the door, which opened straight away. It was the steward.

'You wanted to see me?'

But then he noticed that the count was not there, looked in astonishment at the three people in the room, and beat a retreat, questioning the butler as he arrived outside.

'Soda?' asked Jean Métayer.

And the lawyer, full of good will, began with a little cough:

'We both of us have queer professions, Chief-Inspector ... Have you been in the police force a long time? ... I've been at the bar for nearly fifteen years ... So you can imagine that I've been mixed up in the most astonishing cases ... Good health! ... Here's to you, Monsieur Métayer ... I'm glad for your sake about the turn events are taking ...'

The count could be heard in the corridor saying:

'Well, you must find some! Telephone your son, who is playing billiards in the Café de Paris at Moulins ... He'll bring along what's necessary.'

The door opened. The count came in.

'You've found something to drink? ... Aren't there any cigars here?'

And he looked inquiringly at Métayer.

'Cigarettes ... I only smoke ...'

The young man did not finish what he was saying, but turned his head away in embarrassment.

'I'll bring you some.'

'Gentlemen, I hope you'll excuse the very modest meal

that you're going to eat. We are a long way from the town and ...'

'Come,' said the lawyer, on whom the whisky was beginning to take effect. 'I'm sure it will be excellent ... Is that a portrait of a relative of yours?'

He pointed to a portrait on the wall of the drawing-room, of a man dressed in a stiff frock coat, his neck imprisoned in a starched collar.

'That is my father.'

'Yes, you take after him.'

The servant showed in Doctor Bouchardon who looked around him distrustfully, as if he suspected a drama of some sort. But Saint-Fiacre received him gaily.

'Come in, Doctor ... I presume you know Jean Métayer ... His lawyer ... A charming man, as you'll see ... As for the chief-inspector ...'

The two men shook hands and a few moments later the doctor growled in Maigret's ear:

'What have you cooked up here?'

'I haven't ... It's him!'

To keep himself in countenance, the lawyer kept going to the little table where he had put his glass and he did not realize that he was drinking more than usual.

'This old château is an absolute gem ... And what a setting for a film! ... That's what I was saying only the other day to the Public Prosecutor at Bourges, who loathes the cinema ... As long as they go on shooting films in settings which ...'

He was talking excitedly, and constantly trying to buttonhole somebody.

As for the count, he had gone over to Métayer and was showing a disturbing affability towards him.

'The saddest thing here is the long winter evenings, isn't it? ... *In my time,* I remember that my father too was in the habit of inviting the doctor and the priest ... They weren't the same ones as now ... But the doctor was already a sceptic and the conversation always ended up by turning to philosophical subjects ... And talk of the devil ...'

It was the priest, with rings under his eyes, and an embarrassed expression, who did not know what to say and was standing hesitantly in the doorway.

'Excuse me for being late, but ...'

Through the open doors they could see two servants laying the table in the dining-room.

'Do offer Monsieur le Curé something to drink ...'

It was to Métayer that the count was speaking. Maigret noticed that he himself was not drinking, but the lawyer, for his part, was well on the way to being drunk. He was explaining to the chief-inspector:

'A little diplomacy, that's all! Or, if you like, knowledge of human nature ... They're about the same age, and both from good families ... Can you think of any reasons why they should have failed to hit it off? . . Aren't their interests related? ... The curious thing ...'

He laughed. He took another drink of whisky.

'... is that it happened accidentally in a café ... There's a lot to be said for those good old provincial cafés where you feel as though you were at home ...'

They had heard the sound of a motor outside. A little later the count went into the dining-room, where the steward was, and they caught a few words:

'Both of you, yes! ... If you like! ... That's an order!'

The telephone rang. The count had rejoined his guests. The butler came into the smoking-room.

'The undertaker ... He wants to know when he can bring the coffin ...'

'Whenever he likes.'

'Very well, Monsieur le Comte.'

And the latter said almost gaily:

'Shall we go into dinner? ... I've had the last bottles

in the cellar brought up ... After you, Monsieur le Curé
... We're a little short of feminine company, but ...'

Maigret tried to hold him back by his sleeve. The
other looked him in the eyes with a hint of impatience,
then disengaged himself abruptly and went into the
dining-room.

'I've invited Monsieur Gautier, our steward, and his
son, a young man with a promising future, to share our
meal ...'

Maigret looked at the bank clerk's hair, and, in spite
of his uneasiness, he could not help smiling. The hair was
wet. Before coming to the château, the young man had
checked his parting, washed his face and hands, and
changed his tie.

'Let's sit down, gentlemen.'

And the chief-inspector could have sworn that a sob
rose in Saint-Fiacre's throat. It went unnoticed because
the doctor involuntarily distracted everyone's attention
by seizing a dusty bottle and murmuring:

'So you still have some Hospice de Beaune 1896? ...
I thought that the last bottles had been bought by the
Restaurant Larue and that ...'

The rest was drowned by the sound of the chairs being
moved. The priest, his hands folded on the table-cloth,
his head bent, his lips moving, said grace.

Maigret surprised Saint-Fiacre's gaze fixed intently on
him.

9 A Scene from Scott

The dining-room was the part of the château which had
lost the least of its character, thanks to the carved panel-
ling which lined the walls up to the ceiling. Moreover,
the room was high rather than large, and this made it
not only solemn but gloomy, for guests had the impression of eating at the bottom of a well.

On each panel there were two electric lamps, imita-
tion candles which even had artificial beads of wax.

In the middle of the table, there was a real candle-
holder with seven branches and seven real candles.

The Comte de Saint-Fiacre and Maigret were sitting
face to face, but could only see each other if they strained
their necks to look over the flames.

On the count's right, the priest. On his left, Doctor
Bouchardon. Chance had placed Jean Métayer at one
side of the table, the lawyer at the other side. And next
to the chief-inspector there was the steward on one hand,
Émile Gautier on the other.

The butler occasionally advanced into the light to serve
the guests, but as soon as he took two paces back he was
lost in the shadows, and nothing could be seen of him
but his white-gloved hands.

'Wouldn't you think we were in one of Walter Scott's
novels?'

It was the count who was speaking, in a casual voice.
And yet Maigret pricked up his ears, for he sensed an
underlying meaning, guessed something was going to
begin.

They were only at the *hors d'œuvre*. On the table, all mixed up, there were a score of bottles of red and white wine, clarets and burgundies, and each person helped himself.

'There's only one detail that jars,' Maurice de Saint-Fiacre went on. 'In Walter Scott, the poor old girl up-stairs would suddenly start screaming ...'

For a few seconds, everybody stopped eating and they felt something like a draught of icy air pass by.

'Incidentally, Gautier, has she been left alone?'

The steward swallowed hurriedly, and stammered:

'She ... Yes ... There's nobody in Madame la Comtesse's room ...'

'It can't be very cheerful.'

At that moment a foot pressed hard against Maigret's, but the chief-inspector could not guess whose it was. The table was a round one. Each person could reach the centre. And Maigret's uncertainty was due to continue, for during the evening the little kicks would follow one another with increasing frequency.

'Has she received many callers today?'

It was embarrassing to hear him talking like that of his mother, as if she were alive, and the chief-inspector noticed that Jean Métayer was so upset that he stopped eating and gazed in front of him with eyes which looked more and more haggard.

'Nearly all the local farmers,' replied the steward's deep voice.

Whenever the butler noticed a hand reaching out towards a bottle he would step forward noiselessly. His black arm, with a white glove at the end of it, would appear. The liquid would flow. And all this was done so silently and skilfully that the lawyer, who was already more than a little drunk, admiringly set the operation going three or four times.

He followed in fascination that arm, which did not

even brush against his shoulder. In the end he could not contain himself any longer.

'Marvellous! Butler, you're a wizard, and if I could afford a château, I'd take you into my service ...'

'Well, the château will be up for sale soon, and going cheap ...'

This time Maigret frowned as he looked at Saint-Fiacre, who had spoken in a strange voice which was casual yet a little theatrical. In spite of everything, there was something irritating about these remarks. Were his nerves finally getting on edge? Was this a sinister form of humour?

'Chicken in half-mourning,' he announced as the butler brought in a dish of chicken served with truffles.

And the count went straight on, in the same light-hearted voice:

'The murderer is going to eat some chicken in half-mourning, like the rest of us!'

The butler's arm slipped backwards and forwards between the guests. The steward's voice said in a tone of comic horror:

'Oh, Monsieur le Comte ...'

'Why yes! What is so extraordinary about that? The murderer is here, that's certain! But don't let that take away your appetite, Monsieur le Curé! The corpse is in the house too, and that isn't preventing us from eating ... A little wine, Albert, for Monsieur le Curé!'

The foot brushed against Maigret's ankle again. The chief-inspector dropped his napkin and bent down to look under the table, but too late. When he straightened up again, the count, without stopping eating his chicken, was saying:

'I mentioned Walter Scott just now because of the atmosphere in this room, but also and above all because of the murderer ... After all, this is a funeral wake ... The funeral takes place tomorrow morning and in all probability we shall stay together until then ... It must at least be said to Monsieur Métayer's credit that he has filled the spirits cupboard with some excellent whisky ...'

Maigret tried to remember how much Saint-Fiacre had drunk. Less in any case than the lawyer, who exclaimed:

'Yes, excellent! There's no doubt about that! But then my client is the grandson of some vine-growers ...

'As I was saying ... But what was I saying? ... Oh, yes! ... Fill up Monsieur le Curé's glass, Albert ...

'As I was saying, since the murderer's here, the others find themselves, so to speak, cast in the role of justicers ... And that is what makes our dinner party resemble something out of Walter Scott ...

'Though you must remember that the murderer in question isn't really in any danger. Isn't that so, Chief-Inspector? ... It isn't a crime to slip a piece of paper into a missal ...

'While we are on the subject, Doctor ... When did my mother's last attack take place?'

The doctor wiped his mouth, and looked around him with a disgruntled expression.

'Three months ago, when you wired from Berlin that you were ill in a hotel room and that ...'

'I wanted some cash! That's it!'

'I observed at that time that the next violent shock would be fatal.'

'So that ... Let's see ... Who knew that? ... Jean Métayer, of course ... I myself, obviously ... Old Gautier, who is almost one of the family ... And finally you and Monsieur le Curé ...'

He drank a whole glass of Pouilly and pulled a face.

'This is just to explain to you that logically speaking we can nearly all be considered as suspects ... If the idea amuses you ...'

112

It was as if he were deliberately choosing the most shocking words he could find.

'If the idea amuses you, we can go on to examine the case of each person separately ... Let us begin with Monsieur le Curé ... Had he anything to gain by killing my mother? ... You are going to see that the answer is not as simple as it may appear .. I leave the question of money on one side ...'

The priest was choking with indignation and hesitating whether to leave the table.

'Monsieur le Curé had nothing to hope for in that respect ... But he is a mystic, an apostle, almost a saint ... He has an odd parishioner whose conduct is a source of scandal ... Sometimes she rushes to church like the most fervent of the faithful, but at other times she brings down scandal on Saint-Fiacre ... No, don't make that face, Métayer ... We're all men here ... We are, if you like, engaged in advanced psychology ...

'Monsieur le Curé has such a fierce faith that it might push him to extreme measures. Remember the times when sinners were burnt to purify them ... My mother is at Mass ... She has just taken communion ... She is in a state of grace ... But, very soon, she is going to fall back into her sinful ways and be a source of scandal once more ...

'Whereas if she dies a holy death, there in her pew ...'

'But ...' began the priest, who had big tears in his eyes and who was holding on to the table to keep calm.

'Don't take offence, Monsieur le Curé ... We are simply talking psychology. I want to show you that the most austere people can be suspected of the worst outrages ... If we go on now to the doctor, I'm in a more difficult position ... He isn't a saint ... And, fortunately for him he isn't even a *savant* ... For if he were, he might have put the piece of paper in the missal as an experiment to test the resistance of a weak heart ...'

The sound of forks had slowed down to such an extent that it had nearly dropped to nothing. And the guests' eyes were fixed, uneasy, even haggard. Only the butler was unmoved, and went on filling the glasses in silence, with the regularity of a metronome.

'You look gloomy, gentlemen ... Is it really not possible for us, as intelligent people, to broach certain subjects?

'Serve the next course, Albert ... So we put the doctor on one side, seeing that we cannot regard him as a *savant* or a researcher ... He is saved by his mediocrity ...'

He gave a little laugh and turned towards old Gautier.

'Your turn now ... A more complicated case ... There are two possibilities ... First, you are the model steward, the upright man who devotes his life to his masters and the château where he was born and bred ... You weren't born and bred here, but that doesn't matter ... In this case, your position isn't clear. The Saint-Fiacres have only one male heir ... And the family fortune is rapidly disappearing bit by bit under the nose of that heir ... The countess is behaving like a lunatic ... Isn't it time to save what's left?

'Now that's as noble as anything in Walter Scott, and your case resembles that of Monsieur le Curé ...

'But there's the opposite hypothesis to be considered too! You are no longer the model steward born and bred at the château ... You are a scoundrel and for years you've been taking advantage of your masters' weakness ... When a mortgage is raised, it's you who take it up ... Now don't lose your temper, Gautier ... The Curé didn't lose his, did he? ... And I haven't finished yet ...

'You are practically the real owner of the château ...'

'Monsieur le Comte!'

'Don't you know how to play the game? Because I tell you we are playing a game! We are playing, if you

114

like, at all being chief-inspectors like your neighbour ...
The time has come when the countess has her back to
the wall, everything will have to be sold, and she will
find out that it's you who have profited from the situation ... Wouldn't it be better for the countess to die
conveniently, something which would also save her from
making the acquaintance of poverty?'

And, turning towards the butler, a shadow in the
shadows, a demon with two chalk-white hands, he said:

'Albert! ... Go and fetch my father's revolver ...
That is, of course, if it's still here ...'

He poured out some wine for himself and for his two
neighbours, then passed the bottle to Maigret.

'Will you do the serving on your side? ... Whew!
We've almost got half-way through our little game ...
But let's wait for Albert ... Monsieur Métayer ... You
aren't drinking ...'

They heard a strangled 'No, thank you.'

'How about you, Maître?'

The latter, his mouth full, his tongue coated, replied:

'No, thank you! No, thank you! I've everything I
need ... I say, you'd make a wonderful Advocate General, you know ...'

He was the only one there to laugh, to eat with in-
decent gusto, and to drink glass after glass, sometimes of
burgundy, sometimes of claret, without even noticing the
difference.

They heard the tinny bell of the church clock strike
ten. Albert handed a heavy revolver to the count and the
latter checked that it was loaded.

'Perfect! ... I'll put it here, in the middle of the
table ... You will notice, gentlemen, that as this is a
round table, it is at an equal distance from each person
... We have examined three cases ... Now we are going
to examine three more ... But first of all, will you allow
me to make a prophecy? ... Well, to remain in the

115

Walter Scott tradition, I foretell that before midnight my mother's murderer will be dead!'

Maigret darted a sharp glance at him across the table, and saw a pair of eyes which were shining brightly, as if Saint-Fiacre were drunk. At the same moment a foot touched his again.

'And now I'll go on ... But do eat your salad ... I come now to your neighbour, Chief-Inspector, on your left, that is to say Emile Gautier ... A serious, hard-working young fellow, who, as they say at school speech-days, has made his way by sheer merit and hard work ...

'Could he have killed my mother?

'One hypothesis: he worked hand in glove with his father, for his father ...

'He goes every day to Moulins ... He knows the financial situation of the family better than anybody else ... He has every opportunity of seeing a printer or a linotype operator ...

'Let's go on ... Second hypothesis ... You'll forgive me for telling you, Métayer, if you don't know already, that you had a rival ... Emile Gautier is no beauty ... All the same, he preceded you in the position which you occupied with such tact ...

'That was a few years ago ... Did he begin to entertain certain hopes? ... Had he succeeded, since then, in stirring my mother's tender heart once more?

'The fact remains that he was her official protégé, and that he was entitled to conceive all sorts of ambitions ...

'You came ... You conquered ...

'Why not kill the countess and at the same time throw suspicion on you? ...'

Maigret's toes stirred uncomfortably in his shoes. All this was horrible, sacrilegious! Saint-Fiacre was talking as excitedly as a drunkard. And the others were wondering whether they could stick it out to the end, whether they should stay and endure this scene or get up and go.

116

'You can see that we are faced with a complete mystery ... Mind you, the countess herself, up there, if she could speak, would be unable to give us the solution to the problem. The murderer is the only person who knows about his crime ... Eat up, Emile Gautier ... Above all, don't let this upset you like your father, who seems to be on the verge of fainting ...

'Albert! ... There must be a few bottles of wine left in the bin somewhere ...

'Your turn now, young man!'

And he turned with a smile to face Métayer, who jumped to his feet.

'Monsieur, my lawyer ...'

'Sit down, dammit! And don't make us think that at your age you can't take a joke ...'

Maigret was watching him while he was saying this and he noticed that the count's forehead was covered with big beads of sweat.

'None of us is trying to make himself out to be better than he is, is he? Good! I see that you are beginning to understand. Take some fruit. It's excellent for the digestion ...'

It was unbearably hot and Maigret wondered who had switched off the electric lamps, leaving only the candles on the table burning.

'Your case is so simple that it's positively uninteresting ... You were playing a not very amusing part, which nobody is willing to play for very long ... Still, you were in my mother's will ... That will risked being changed at any moment ... A sudden death and it would be all over! You would be free! You would harvest the fruits of your ... of your sacrifice ... And, dammit all, you would be able to marry some young girl whom you must have waiting for you back home ...'

'I beg your pardon!' the lawyer protested, so comically that Maigret could not help smiling.

117

'Shut your trap! Drink up!'

Saint-Fiacre was categorical! He was drunk, there could no longer be any shadow of a doubt about that! He was displaying that eloquence peculiar to drunkards, a mixture of brutality and subtlety, of facile eloquence and blurred speech.

'I'm the only one left!'

He called Albert.

'Look, old chap, go upstairs ... It must be so dismal for my mother, staying all alone ...'

Maigret saw the butler glance inquiringly at old Gautier, who gave a little nod.

'Just a moment! Bring us a few bottles first ... The whisky too ... Nobody objects to a little informality, I imagine ...'

He looked at his watch.

'Ten past eleven ... I've been talking such a lot that I haven't heard your church clock, Monsieur le Curé ...'

And, as the butler moved the revolver slightly while putting the whisky decanters on the table, the count said:

'Careful, Albert! ... It must remain at an equal distance from each of us ...'

He waited until the door was closed.

'There!' he said. 'I'm the only one left! I won't be telling you anything new when I say I've never done anything worthwhile. Except perhaps in my father's lifetime ... But seeing that he died when I was only seventeen ...

'I'm on the rocks ... Everybody knows that ... The popular weeklies make no secret of the fact ...

'I sign dud cheques ... I try my mother for a touch as often as I can ... I invent the illness in Berlin to get a few thousand francs ...

'You will notice that that was the missal trick on a smaller scale ...

'Now, what's happening? ... The money which is due to come to me some day is being spent by little swines

118

like Métayer ... Excuse me, old fellow ... This is still transcendental psychology ...

'Soon there'll be nothing left ... I telephone to my mother, at a time when a dud cheque is just about to land me in prison ... She refuses to pay ... There are witnesses who can testify to that ...

'Besides, if this goes on, there'll be nothing left of the family fortune in a few weeks ...

'Two hypotheses, as in the case of Emile Gautier. The first ...'

Never in his whole career had Maigret felt so uncomfortable. And it was probably the first time he had had the definite impression of being incapable of dealing with the situation. Events were leaving him behind. Now and then he thought he understood, and the next moment a phrase of Saint-Fiacre's would call everything in question again.

And all the time there was that insistent foot pressing against his.

'Let's change the subject!' suggested the lawyer, who was now completely drunk.

'Gentlemen,' began the priest.

'I beg your pardon! You must bear with me until midnight at least! I was saying that the first hypothesis ...

'Damn! Now you've made me lose the thread of my ideas ...'

And, as if to help him find it again, he poured himself a full glass of whisky.

'I know that my mother is very tender-hearted. I slip the piece of paper into her missal, in order to frighten her and thus soften her up, with the intention of coming back the next day to ask her for the necessary sum, in the hope of finding her more sympathetic ...

'But there's the second hypothesis! Why shouldn't I too want to kill her?

119

'Not all the Saint-Fiacre fortune has gone. There's a little money left. And in my position a little money, however little, may make all the difference.

'I am vaguely aware that Métayer is mentioned in the will. But a murderer can't inherit ...

'Isn't he the man everyone will suspect of the crime? He who spends part of his time in a printing-house at Moulins? He who, living in the château, can slip the piece of paper into the missal whenever he likes?

'Didn't I arrive at Moulins on Saturday afternoon? And didn't I wait there with my mistress, for the result of this operation?'

He stood up, his glass in his hand.

'Your good health, gentlemen ... You look gloomy ... The whole of my mother's poor life, these last few years, was gloomy ... Isn't that so, Monsieur le Curé? ... It's only fair that her last night should be accompanied by a little gaiety ...'

He looked the chief-inspector in the eyes.

'Your good health, Monsieur Maigret!'

He was making fun of somebody, but of whom? Of himself? Of everybody else?

Maigret felt that he was confronted by a force against which there was nothing to be done. Certain individuals, at a given moment in their lives, have an hour of fulfilment like this, an hour during which they are, as it were, situated above the rest of mankind and above themselves.

Such is the case of the gambler who, at Monte Carlo, wins all the time, whatever he does. Such is the case of the hitherto unknown member of the Opposition who, with a speech he makes, brings down the government, and is the first to be surprised, since all that he wanted was a few lines in the parliamentary reports.

Maurice de Saint-Fiacre was living this hour. There was a strength in him which he himself had never guessed at before, and the others could do nothing but bow their heads.

But wasn't it drink which was carrying him away like that?

'Let's go back to the starting-point of our conversation, gentlemen, seeing that it isn't midnight yet ... I have said that my mother's murderer was here among us ... I have proved that he could be myself or any one of you, except perhaps the chief-inspector and the doctor.

'I'm not even sure of that ...

'And I have prophesied his death ...

'Will you allow me to play the hypothesis game once again? He knows that the Law is powerless against him. But he also knows that there are, or rather will be, a few persons, six at least, who know about his crime ...

'There again, we are faced with several solutions ...

'The first is the most romantic, the most consistent with the spirit of Walter Scott ...

'But here I must open a fresh parenthesis ... What is the distinguishing feature of this crime? ... It is that there are at least five individuals who were revolving around the countess ... Five individuals who stood to benefit by her death, and each of whom may have envisaged the means of bringing about that death ...

'Only one dared ... Only one killed ...

'Well, gentlemen, I can easily imagine that individual taking advantage of this dinner-party to revenge himself on the others ... He is done for! ... Why not blow us all up?'

And Maurice de Saint-Fiacre, with a disarming smile, looked at each guest in turn.

'Isn't it fascinating? The old dining-room of the old château, the candles, the table loaded with bottles ... Then, at midnight, death ... You will note that at the same time all possibilities of scandal would be averted ... Tomorrow, people would find us and be completely baffled ... They would talk of an accident or of an anarchist plot ...'

The lawyer stirred on his chair and glanced anxiously around him, into the darkness which began less than a yard from the table.

'If I may venture to recall that I am a doctor,' growled Bouchardon, 'I would recommend a cup of strong black coffee for everybody ...'

'And I,' the priest said slowly, 'would remind you that there is a dead person in the house ...'

Saint-Fiacre hesitated for a moment. A foot brushed against Maigret's ankle, and he bent down quickly, but once again too late.

'I asked you to give me until midnight ... I have only examined the first hypothesis ... There is another ... The murderer, hunted down, panic-stricken, blows out his brains ... *But I don't think he will do that* ...'

'For God's sake let's go into the smoking-room!' yelped the lawyer, standing up and hanging on to the back of his chair to avoid falling.

'Finally, there is a third hypothesis ... Somebody who cares for the honour of the family comes to the murderer's help ... Wait a moment ... The question is more complicated than that ... Mustn't a scandal be avoided at all costs? ... Mustn't the culprit be *helped* to commit suicide?

'The revolver is there, gentlemen, at an equal distance from every hand .. It is ten to twelve ... I repeat that at midnight the murderer will be dead ...'

And this time he spoke so emphatically that nobody said a word. Everyone held his breath.

'The victim is up there, watched over by a servant ... The murderer is here, surrounded by seven people ...'

Saint-Fiacre drained his glass at one draught and the anonymous foot went on brushing against Maigret's foot.

'Six minutes to twelve ... Isn't this just like Walter

Scott? I trust the murderer is beginning to shake in his shoes . . .'

He was drunk, but he went on drinking.

'Five people at least with reason to rob an old woman deprived of her husband and starved of love . . . Only one who dared . . . It will be a bomb or a revolver, gentlemen . . . A bomb which will blow us all up, or a revolver which will kill only the culprit . . . Four minutes to twelve . . .'

And he added in a curt voice:

'Don't forget that nobody knows!'

He seized the bottle of whisky and served everybody, beginning with Maigret's glass and finishing with Emile Gautier's.

He did not fill up his own . . . Hadn't he drunk enough? One candle went out. The others were on the point of following suit.

'I said midnight . . . Three minutes to twelve . . .'

He was talking like an auctioneer.

'Three minutes to twelve . . . Two minutes . . . The murderer is going to die . . . You can begin saying your prayer, Monsieur le Curé . . . As for you, doctor, I trust you've brought your bag with you? . . . Two minutes to twelve . . . One and a half minutes . . .'

And all the time that insistent foot against Maigret's foot. He did not dare to bend down again for fear of missing something else.

'I'm off!' exclaimed the lawyer getting up.

All eyes turned towards him. He was standing up, gripping the back of his chair. He hesitated about venturing on the three dangerous steps which would take him to the door. He hiccoughed.

And at the same moment a shot rang out. There was one second, perhaps two, of general immobility.

A second candle went out, and at the same time Maurice de Saint-Fiacre swayed, hit the back of his

Gothic chair with his shoulders, leaned to the left, tried to regain his balance, but slumped to the floor in an inert mass, with his head on the priest's arm.

10 The Funeral Wake

The scene which followed was confusion. Something was happening everywhere, and afterwards nobody could have described anything but the small part of the events which he had seen himself.

Only five candles were left to light the whole dining-room. Huge areas remained in darkness, and, as they moved about, people walked in and out of them as if they were the wings of a theatre.

The man who had fired was one of Maigret's neighbours: Emile Gautier. And the shot had scarcely rung out before he held his two wrists out towards the chief-inspector in a rather theatrical gesture.

Maigret was standing. Gautier got up. His father too. And the three of them formed a group on one side of the table while another group gathered round the victim.

The Comte de Saint-Fiacre was still lying with his forehead against the priest's arm. The doctor had bent down and then looked around him with a grim expression.

'Is he dead?' asked the plump lawyer.

No reply. It was as if, in that group, the action was being played out limply by bad actors.

There was only Jean Métayer who belonged to neither group. He had remained by his chair, trembling and uneasy, and he did not know where to look.

During the minutes preceding his action, Emile Gautier must have decided what attitude to adopt, for he had scarcely put the weapon back on the table before he literally made a declaration, looking Maigret in the eyes.

'He said what was going to happen himself, didn't he? ... The murderer had to die ... And since he was too cowardly to do justice to himself ...'

His self-assurance was extraordinary.

'I did what I considered to be my duty ...'

Could the others, on the other side of the table, hear? There were some footsteps in the corridor. It was the servants. And the doctor went to the door to prevent them from coming in. Maigret did not hear what he said to them to get rid of them.

'I saw Saint-Fiacre prowling round the château on the night of the crime ... That was how I understood ...'

The whole scene was badly organized. And Gautier was hamming terribly when he declared:

'The judges will say whether ...'

The doctor's voice could be heard asking:

'You're sure that it was Saint-Fiacre who killed his mother?'

'Positive! Would I have done what I have done if ...'

'You saw him prowling round the château on the night before the crime?'

'I saw him as clearly as I can see you now. He had left his car just outside the village ...'

'You've no other proof?'

'Yes, I have! This afternoon the choirboy came to see me at the bank with his mother ... It was his mother who made him talk ... Shortly after the crime, the count asked the boy to give him the missal and promised him some money ...'

Maigret's patience was nearly exhausted, for he had the impression of being left out of the play.

Yes, a play! Why was the doctor smiling into his beard? And why was the priest gently pushing Saint-Fiacre's head away?

A play, moreover, which was to continue on a note of farce and drama combined.

126

For the Comte de Saint-Fiacre was standing up like a man who had just had a nap. The expression in his eyes was hard, and there was an ironic but threatening crease at the corner of his mouth.

'Come here and say that again!' he said.

The cry which rang out was blood-curdling. Emile Gautier was screaming with fear and hanging on to Maigret's arm as if to ask him for protection. But the chief-inspector drew back, leaving the field clear to the two men.

There was somebody who did not understand: Jean Métayer. And he was almost as frightened as the bank clerk. To cap everything, the candle-holder fell over and the tablecloth started smouldering, giving off a smell of burning.

It was the lawyer who prevented the fire from taking hold, by emptying a bottle of wine over it.

'Come here!'

It was an order. And the tone in which it was given was such that they all knew that there was no disobeying it.

Maigret had seized the revolver. A single glance had shown him that it was loaded with blanks.

The rest he could guess. Maurice de Saint-Fiacre letting his head fall against the priest's arm ... A few whispered words asking for the illusion of his death to be preserved for a moment ...

Now he was no longer the same man. He seemed taller, sturdier. He did not take his eyes off young Gautier, and it was the steward who suddenly ran towards a window, opened it and shouted to his son:

'This way!'

It was not a bad plan. The confusion and excitement were so great that at that moment Gautier had a good chance of making his escape.

Did the little lawyer do it on purpose? Probably not.

127

Or else it was drunkenness which invested him with a sort of heroism. As the fugitive was making for the window, he stretched out one leg and Gautier fell headlong.

He did not get up by himself. A hand had seized him by the collar, was lifting him up and putting him on his feet. And he screamed again as he saw that it was Saint-Fiacre who was forcing him to stay upright.

'Don't move! ... Somebody shut the window ...'

And he slammed his fist for the first time into his companion's face, which turned crimson. He did it coldly.

'Now talk! ... Tell us all about it ...'

Nobody intervened. Nobody even thought of doing so, they were so convinced that only one man had the right to raise his voice.

There was only old Gautier to growl in Maigret's ear:

'Are you going to let him do as he likes?'

Yes, he was! Maurice de Saint-Fiacre was in command of the situation, and he was adequate to his task.

'You saw me on the night in question, that's true enough ...'

Then he said to the others:

'Do you know where? ... On the steps ... I was going in ... He was coming out ... I was planning to take some of the family jewels to sell them ... We found ourselves face to face in the dark ... It was freezing ... And this little swine told me that he had just come from ... Have you guessed? Yes, from my mother's bedroom!'

In a lower voice he added casually:

'I abandoned my plan. I went back to Moulins.'

Jean Métayer had opened his eyes wide. The lawyer was stroking his chin, to keep himself in countenance, and kept glancing towards his glass which he did not dare to go and get.

'That wasn't proof enough ... For there were two of them in the house and Gautier could have been telling the truth ... As I explained just now, he was the first to take advantage of an old woman's unhappiness ... Métayer only came along later ... Perhaps Métayer, conscious that his position was threatened, had tried to take his revenge ... I tried to find out ... Both of them were on their guard ... It was as if they were defying me to do anything ...

'That's true, isn't it, Gautier? ... I was the gentleman with the dud cheques who prowled round the château at night, and who wouldn't dare to make any accusations, for fear of getting arrested himself ...'

And in another tone of voice he went on:

'Forgive me, Monsieur le Curé, and you too, Doctor, for inflicting all this filth on you ... But as we've already been told, real justice, the justice of the courts, is powerless here ... That's so, isn't it, Monsieur Maigret? ... Did you understand, at least, when I was kicking you under the table just now?'

He was walking up and down, passing from the light into the shadows and from the shadows into the light. He gave the impression of a man holding himself back and only managing to remain calm at the cost of a tremendous effort. Sometimes he went close enough to Gautier to touch him.

'What a temptation to pick up the revolver and fire! Yes, I had said myself that the culprit would die at midnight and you, you became the defender of the honour of the Saint-Fiacres.'

This time his fist struck so hard, right in the middle of the face, that the bank clerk's nose began bleeding profusely.

Emile Gautier had the eyes of a dying animal. He reeled under the blow and looked as if he was on the point of weeping with pain, fear, and panic.

The lawyer tried to intervene, but Saint-Fiacre pushed him away.

'*You* keep out of this!'

And that *you* emphasized the enormous distance which separated them. Maurice de Saint-Fiacre dominated the company.

'Excuse me, gentlemen, but I have another little formality to see to.'

He opened the door wide and turned towards Gautier.

'Come along!'

The other stood rooted to the ground. The corridor was in darkness. He did not want to go out there with his adversary.

It did not take long. Saint-Fiacre went up to him and hit him again, so hard that he was knocked headlong into the hall.

'Up there!'

And he pointed to the staircase leading to the first floor.

'Chief-Inspector! I warn you that ...' panted the steward.

The priest had turned his head away. He was suffering. But he had not the strength to intervene. Everybody was at the end of his tether and Métayer poured himself a drink, not caring what it was, he was so parched.

'Where are they going?' asked the lawyer.

They could hear them walking along the corridor, whose flagstones rang with the sound of their footsteps. And they could hear Gautier panting for breath.

'You knew everything,' Maigret said slowly, in a very low voice, to the steward. 'You were working hand in glove, you and your son! You already had the farms, the mortgages ... But Jean Métayer remained a risk ... So you decided to kill the countess, and at the same time get rid of the gigolo who would fall under suspicion ...'

A cry of pain. The doctor went into the corridor to see what was happening.

'It's nothing,' he said. 'The little swine doesn't want to go upstairs and he's being helped along.'

130

'This is a scandal! ... It's a crime! ... What is he going to do?' cried old Gautier, rushing out of the room.

Maigret and the doctor followed him. They arrived at the foot of the staircase just as the other two, upstairs, reached the door of the dead woman's bedroom.

And they heard Saint-Fiacre's voice:

'In you go!'

'I can't ... I ...'

'In you go!'

A dull thud. Another blow.

Old Gautier ran up the stairs, followed by Maigret and Bouchardon. All three arrived at the top just as the door was closing.

At first they could hear nothing behind the heavy oak door. The steward held his breath, grimacing in the dark.

A thin ray of light under the door.

'On your knees!'

A pause. A hoarse gasp.

'Quicker than that! ... On your knees! ... And now beg her forgiveness!'

A fresh silence which was very prolonged. A cry of pain. This time it was not a punch which the murderer had received but a kick full in the face.

'For ... forgive me ...'

'Is that all? ... Is that all you can find to say? ... Remember that it was she who paid for your studies ...

'Forgive me!'

'Remember that three days ago she was alive.'

'Forgive me!'

'Remember, you dirty little swine, that you once wormed your way into her bed ...'

'Forgive me! ... Forgive me!'

'You can do better than that! ... Come, now! ... Tell her you are a filthy louse ... Repeat after me ...'

'I am ...'

'On your knees, I said! ... Do you need a carpet?'

'Don't! ... I ...'

'Beg her forgiveness ...'

And suddenly these exchanges, which were separated by long silences, were followed by a series of loud noises. Saint-Fiacre had lost his self-control. There were a number of thuds on the floor.

Maigret opened the door a little way. Maurice de Saint-Fiacre was holding Gautier by the neck and banging his head on the ground.

When he saw the chief-inspector, he let go, wiped his forehead, and straightened up.

'I've finished,' he said, breathing fast.

He caught sight of the steward and frowned.

'Don't you feel the need to beg her forgiveness too?'

And the old man was so frightened that he threw himself on his knees.

All that they could see of the dead woman, in the dim light from a couple of tapers, was the nose which seemed enormous and the folded hands which were holding a rosary.

'Get out!'

The count pushed Emile Gautier out of the room and shut the door. And the group started going downstairs.

Emile Gautier was bleeding. He could not find his handkerchief. The doctor passed him his.

For the bank clerk was a horrible sight: a battered, blood-stained face, with the nose nothing but a tumour and the upper lip split open ...

And yet the ugliest, the most horrifying thing about his appearance was the eyes with their shifty expression ...

Maurice de Saint-Fiacre, very upright, like the master of a house who knows what he has to do, strode along the long ground-floor corridor and opened the door, letting in a gust of icy air.

'Get out!' he growled, turning toward the father and son.

132

But, just as Emile was going out, he caught hold of him with an instinctive gesture.

Maigret was certain that he heard a sob in the count's throat. He started hitting the bank clerk again, convulsively, and crying:

'You swine! ... You swine!'

It was enough for the chief-inspector just to touch him on the shoulder. Saint-Fiacre regained his composure, literally threw the body down the steps, and shut the door.

But not before they had heard the old man's voice again:

'Emile ... Where are you?'

*

The priest was praying, with his elbows on the sideboard. In one corner Métayer and his lawyer were sitting motionless, their eyes fixed on the door.

Maurice de Saint-Fiacre came in, his head held high

'Gentlemen,' he began.

But he could not go on. His voice was choked by emotion. He was at the end of his tether.

He shook hands with the doctor and Maigret, as much as to say they could now go. Then, turning towards Métayer and his companion, he waited.

Those two did not seem to understand. Or else they were paralysed with fear.

To show them the way, a gesture was required, followed by a snap of the fingers.

That was all.

Or was it? The lawyer started looking for his hat, and Saint-Fiacre groaned:

'Quicker than that!'

Maigret heard a murmur of voices behind a door, and he guessed that it was the servants who were there, trying to puzzle out what was happening in the château.

He put on his heavy overcoat. He felt the need to shake hands once more with Saint-Fiacre.

The door was open. Outside, it was a bright cold night, without a single cloud. The poplars stood out against a moonlit sky. Foosteps rang out somewhere, a long way away. And there were lights in the windows of the steward's house.

'No, you stay, Monsieur le Curé ...'

And in the echoing corridor Maurice de Saint-Fiacre's voice added:

'Now, if you are not too tired, we are going to watch over my mother ...'

11 The Whistle

'You mustn't be cross with me, Monsieur Maigret, for looking after you so badly ... But what with the funeral ...'

Poor Marie Tatin was bustling around, getting whole crates of beer and lemonade ready.

'Especially seeing that those who live a long way off will drop in here for a bite ...'

The fields were white with frost and the grass crackled underfoot. Every quarter of an hour the passing-bell of the little church tolled.

The hearse had arrived at dawn and the undertaker's men were waiting at the inn, in a half circle round the stove.

'I'm surprised the steward isn't at home,' Marie Tatin had told them. 'He's probably at the château with Monsieur Maurice ...'

Already a few peasants could be seen, who had put on their Sunday clothes.

Maigret was finishing his breakfast when, through the window, he saw the choirboy arrive, holding his mother's hand. But the woman did not accompany him as far as the inn. She stopped at the corner on the road, where she thought she was out of sight, and pushed her son forward, as if to give him the necessary impetus to reach Marie Tatin's inn.

When Ernest came in, he was very self-assured. As self-assured as a boy who, at his school speech-day, recites a fable he has been rehearsing for three months.

'Is the chief-inspector here?'

At the very moment he was asking Marie Tatin this question, he caught sight of Maigret and came towards him, with both hands in his pockets, and one of them toying with something.

'I've come to ...'

'Show me your whistle.'

Ernest promptly took a step back, turned his eyes away, thought for a moment, and murmured:

'What whistle?'

'The one you've got in your pocket ... Have you been wanting a boy-scout whistle for a long time?'

The boy took it automatically from his pocket and put it on the table.

'And now tell me your little story.'

A suspicious glance, followed by an imperceptible shrug of the shoulders. For Ernest was already cunning. The expression in his eyes said clearly:

'I don't care! I've got the whistle! I'm going to say what I was told to say ...'

And he recited:

'It's about the missal ... I didn't tell you everything the other day, because I was scared of you ... But Ma wants me to tell the truth ... Somebody came and asked me for the missal, just before High Mass ...'

All the same, he was red in the face, and he snatched the whistle back as if he were afraid of having it confiscated because of his lie.

'And who came and asked you for it?'

'Monsieur Métayer ... The secretary at the château ...'

'Come and sit next to me ... Would you like a grenadine?'

'Yes ... With fizzy water ...'

'Bring us a grenadine with soda water, Marie ... And you, are you pleased with your whistle? ... Blow it for me ...'

136

The undertaker's men turned round as they heard the whistle.

'Your mother bought it for you yesterday afternoon, didn't she?'

'How do you know?'

'How much did they give her yesterday at the bank?'

The boy looked him in the eyes. He was no longer red in the face but pale. He glanced towards the door, as if to see how far he was from it.

'Drink your grenadine ... It was Emile Gautier who saw you ... He taught you what to say ...'

'Yes!'

'He told you to accuse Jean Métayer?'

'Yes.'

And, after a pause for thought:

'What are you going to do to me?'

Maigret forgot to reply. He was thinking. He was thinking that his part in this case had been limited to finding the last link, a tiny link which completed the chain.

It was Jean Métayer all right whom Gautier had wanted to have accused. But the previous evening had upset his plans. He had realized that the man he had to fear was not the secretary, but the Comte de Saint-Fiacre.

If all had gone well, he would have been obliged to go to see the red-haired boy again before long, to teach him a new lesson:

'You must say that it was Monsieur le Comte who asked you for the missal ...'

And now the boy repeated:

'What are you going to do to me?'

Maigret did not have time to reply. The lawyer came down the stairs, entered the main room of the inn, and approached Maigret, his hand outstretched, with a hint of hesitation.

'Did you sleep well, Chief-Inspector? ... Excuse me ... I would like to ask your advice, on behalf of my client ... I've such a terrible headache ...'

He sat down, or rather slumped on the bench.

'The funeral is at ten o'clock, isn't it?'

He looked at the undertaker's men, then at the people passing along the road, waiting for the funeral to begin.

'Between ourselves, do you think that Métayer's duty is to ... Don't misunderstand me ... We understand the situation and it's precisely out of a sense of delicacy that ...'

'Can I go now, Monsieur?'

Maigret did not hear. He was talking to the lawyer.

'Haven't you understood yet?'

'I mean if one examines ...'

'Let me give you a piece of advice: don't examine anything at all!'

'In your opinion it would be better to leave without ...?'

Too late! Ernest, who had recovered his whistle, had opened the door and taken to his heels.

'From the legal point of view, we are in an excellent position ...'

'Yes, excellent!'

'Isn't it? ... That's what I was saying to ...'

'Did he sleep well?'

'He didn't even undress ... He's a very highly-strung, very sensitive fellow, like many young men of good family and ...'

But the undertaker's men were pricking up their ears, standing up, paying for their drinks. Maigret stood up too, took his overcoat with the velvet collar from the coatstand, and wiped his bowler hat with his sleeve.

'The two of you have a chance to slip away during ...'

'During the funeral? ... In that case, I must telephone for a taxi.'

'That's it ...'

*

The priest in his surplice. Ernest and two other choir-boys in their black cassocks. The cross which a priest from a nearby village was carrying, walking fast because of the cold. And the liturgical chants which they were intoning as they hurried along the road.

The peasants were grouped at the foot of the steps. Nothing could be seen inside. Finally the door opened and the coffin appeared, carried by four men.

Behind, a tall silhouette. Maurice de Saint-Fiacre, red-eyed, very erect.

He was not in black. He was the only person not wearing mourning.

And yet, when, from the top of the steps, he let his gaze wander over the crowd, there was, as it were, a feeling of embarrassment.

He came out of the château with no one beside him. And he followed the coffin alone . . .

From where he was, Maigret could see the steward's house which had been his own home, and whose doors and windows were closed.

The shutters of the château were closed too. Only in the kitchen some servants had their noses pressed against the window-panes.

The sound of sacred chants almost drowned by the crunch of footsteps on the gravel.

The bells in full peal.

Two pairs of eyes met: the count's and Maigret's.

Was the chief-inspector mistaken? It seemed to him that Maurice de Saint-Fiacre's lips were touched by the ghost of a smile. Not the smile of the sceptical Parisian, the penniless prodigal.

A serene, confident smile . . .

During the Mass, everybody heard the high-pitched horn of a taxi. A little swine was making his escape in the company of a lawyer with a hangover.

More about Penguins
and Pelicans

Simenon

Maigret Stonewalled

A simple enough case . . . on the face of it. A commercial traveller killed in a hotel bedroom on the Loire. But Maigret sensed falseness everywhere, in the way the witnesses spoke and laughed and acted and, above all, in the manner of M. Gallet's death.

And behind the falseness, as Maigret discovered, the pathos of a man for whom nothing had ever gone right – not even death.

Maigret and the Enigmatic Lett

Pietr the Lett had for years been clocked across the European frontiers by Interpol. Who was he, this international swindler with the skin of a chameleon? Was he Oswald Oppenheim, friend of multi-millionaires? Or Olaf Swann, a Norwegian merchant officer down at Fécamp? Or Féder Yurovich, a down-and-out Russian drunk? Or could he have been the twisted corpse they found on the Pole Star express when it drew into Paris?

It cost Maigret one of his best inspectors – and a ducking in the sea – to unravel one of the most tortuous puzzles of identity he had ever handled.

Simenon

Maigret At The Crossroads

Translated from *La Nuit du Carrefour*, this is the story of Maigret's classic vigil at the crossroads. An unforgettable night, vibrating like a concert grand with action and tension.

Twenty miles south of Paris they found the corpse of a Jewish diamond-merchant from Antwerp. Nobody knew him. Then the diamond-merchant's widow was shot down in the dark at Maigret's feet, and the chief inspector plunged into action like a wounded buffalo, as ponderous, as merciless, and as cunning.

Maigret Meets a Milord

One of the canal carters stumbled on the corpse of Mary Lampson, strangled in a stable near the lock: the find plunged Maigret into the damp world of barges and towpath cafés.

It called for a chase on a bicycle and a confession from a dying man to draw together all the strands of a curious and pitiful story.

Also available:
Maigret and the Hundred Gibbets

Maigret Mystified

Maigret's First Case *and*

Sailor's Rendezvous